GODFREY

GODFREY

FANNING

CHAPTER 1:

I shoved open the doors. Frigid air curled through the gap before the glass rattled shut again. Flynt's sandals snapped against the cracked, off-white tiles, while I dug my hands deeper into my jacket. The floor squelched beneath my boots, sticky in patches, soft in others. Above, the light fluttered with the gray mold that drizzled down the walls. The shelves, black with peeling white rust, leaned into the aisle, their edges glinting with dampness. A puddle spread between two racks, thick and yellow; my boot tapped it, sending ripples skittering. The residue clung to my sole, dragging streams along the tiles.

I kicked a can into the wall. "You'll love this—uh—they've got cool shit. Still ugly as fuck in this…shithole."

Flynt gave a half-nod. "I don't know what that means, Avery."

"Hey—it's just close, and… Um… It'll be a nice rest stop before I drop you off. Fuck you." My thumb hooked the edge of my waistband. The jacket hem bunched around my hips.

Trash caked the floor—crumpled chip bags, lottery tickets, and cigarette packs floating in shallow puddles. The scent of musty wood and gasoline churned within my throat. Beetles crowded the shelves, legs clicking over the rusted metal.

I grimaced back through the streaked glass; my car sat across two spaces, its headlights dimming in the drizzle, a dark contour against the gas pumps' faded glow. Beyond it, houses sagged into the rain, roofs caved, windows gaping.

"Shit," I said. "I left my—uh—you know…"

"Gun," Flynt said.

I shushed him.

Flynt stopped at the end of the aisle, his shadow breaking jagged over the wall. Black mold bulged there, brittle and swollen, edges fraying—burned paper. Threads of it streaked, pooled at the base of the shelves.

The puddle near my feet quivered, rippling outward from a faint tremor deeper in the station. The buzzing light overhead dimmed, flickering sharp shadows onto the walls. Flynt glanced back, hair falling over his eyes—loose, still.

"Should I just…run back and get it?" I asked. He shrugged; his loose shirt sagged and heaved in the stale air, beige fabric puffing across his shoulder. I scratched my temple. "I guess we're fucking paying… Uh, I probably wasn't gonna drag out the piece over some snacks." Flynt slowly turned out his empty pockets, pulled the lining out, then dropped it all back in. His eyes drifted upward, locking on the dim ceiling lights. I sighed. My shoulders snapped up, then dropped heavy. "Don't haul ass. I'm broke until my check clears."

The shelves loomed, half-stripped. My gaze snagged on the chips: black bags crinkled and slumped against each other. My hand darted out. The metal rack screeched as I tore a chip bag free. Black grit flaked off, falling in jagged crumbs to the floor. The white, cartoonish rabbit logo grinned, stirring with a fractured spiral of color on black gloss. The black on its surface was pure, seamless, and it was warm in my hands. I tilted it against the fluorescent light—hot, viscous fluid sloshed inside the bag. I shook it up, popped it into the air, and caught it; the bag crinkled under my grip. Its surface was slick, leaving a faint smear on my palm. I squeezed tighter. The printed shapes warped under the pressure.

"Hey…uh… There used to be—fuck, I don't know—stuff. They had these goo-ass snack cakes."

I strode down the narrow aisle, boots thudding against the grimy tiles. The air tasted stale. Flynt stood by the shelf, motionless; he glanced over, then resumed scanning the aisles. There were boxes and plastic containers lined against the length of the shelf, with dull, peeling labels—smudged, some fallen off—muted beside the glaring pop of the bags.

"Flynt. This shit. Uh—have you tried it?" I asked, nudging his arm.

"Maybe," he mumbled.

"The fuck does that mean?"

The coolers embraced the back wall, rows of drinks uniform behind fogged glass. Flynt approached, the steps disturbing the settled dust, sending tiny puffs spiraling into the air. His shadow was long and thin against the orange glow. He pulled the door open with a limp jerk, the hinges silent. Mist spilled out, an exhale that frosted the air.

Rows of drinks stood at attention. Glass clinked as he pulled one bottle free. A replacement slid forward as the door closed with a soft click. Bold black text printed Yamagzhal across the stark white label.

Beside me, Flynt paused, a beam of light cutting through the murk to draw a faint line across his shirt, dust motes twisting in its path. He edged past, his shoulder grazing mine as he slid into the aisle.

The wind battered the walls, rattling the windows. Flynt turned the drink in his palm—a cold weight, the damp label glinting in the faint light. Frost fogged the bottle, clinging to the ridges as his thumb brushed the cap.

"Okay—now it's fucking cold. Is this your fault? What the fuck, Flynt?" I tugged my jacket tighter across my chest. The lining scratched against my throat.

"What?"

A cracked fixture flickered overhead. The aisle narrowed; the air turned cold. My breath hung in front of me, curling before vanishing. I scanned the shelves. Dust lined the edges, thicker in the corners. My lungs tightened; the cold pressed deeper. The low hum of the coolers along the back wall crawled between us.

He stared, blinked, then set his eyes on the drink. Moisture streaked his smooth skin, beading along the bottle. The floor buzzed; a drip struck somewhere above. I shoved the bag tighter under my arm. A cold draft slid through the shelves, brushing my side. My gaze flicked to Flynt. His grip was still.

A white moth, stark against the dimness of the gas station, fluttered to a halt on the surface of my bag. Its delicate wings beat once, twice, before launching back into the stale air, skimming past Flynt. It disappeared toward the coolers, drawn by the faint orange glow that bled from beneath.

I watched it go. *Yamagzhal:* the name stamped the bag in bold, jagged letters, stark white on black. I flipped it over. The same word stared back. My fingers traced the jagged lines of the cartoon face.

The colors bled together, murky and rotten. I let my arm fall; the bag nestled at my waist, its plastic rustling against my coat.

I squinted at the back of the shelf, where a white, fuzzy slab of meat looked seared to the rack. Decay wafted down the row; thick black maggots swarmed inside of it, pulsing across its surface, leaving a gooey black resin running down its side, dripping down, plopping onto the floor. I reached across the aisle, carefully flicking one maggot off the slab, smirking as it vanished into the darkness. The racks were islands floating in the abyss.

The air clung to my skin, thick with mold and gasoline. Breath gnawed at my lungs. A chip crunched beneath me; shards of glass stuck to my boots, grinding loose as I stepped. The slick surface of the bag slid against my palm. I clenched it tighter, gaze locked on the eyes of the pristine logos lining the aisles. Flynt's vacant eyes met mine, dropped to the bag, then rose again.

My boots struck the damp tiles as I turned. The rain had stopped. Outside, the windows framed nothing—no streetlights, no street. At the back of the store, a hallway stretched into the dark, its edge swallowing the light. A rusted elevator sat behind a sagging mesh door, the metal blotched and bent.

"It's late now," Flynt said. "They're dimming it again."

"Shut the fuck up. What the fuck are you talking about?" I raked my fingers through my hair, eyes squirming across the pane. "Hey— your fucking lights are busted. Somebody fix this shit." I scratched at my jacket hem. "Wait—fuck—my headlights."

My hand brushed a cold rack. Frigid metal bit into my fingers. The surface was slick. I jerked back. Flynt lingered, his gaze locked on the gaping corridor.

A light across the room flickered to life, revealing a broad wooden counter. A woman stood hunched over it, glancing around frantically, her gaze settling faintly onto us. We neared the ledge, the tiles sticking with every step. The lights cast pale, uneven pools across the surface.

A speaker overhead crackled to life, faint and choppy, spilling garbled rock into the glassy air. The floor clung to my boots, peeling free in slimy jerks. The air shifted, tangled in a syrupy rot.

"Uh…been having a hard time quitting—" a woman's voice cut in under the static—stuck in the coil, flattened against the buzz.

Flynt's sandals scuffed beside me before the counter, scratched and stained. Its wooden surface was a long semicircle, light, marbled, and sticky. Beyond the attendant was nothing but darkness, the room disappearing into a fathomless void.

I slammed my bag onto the counter, its wet insides sloshing; in parallel, Flynt left his thick, black glass on the counter with a casual toss, shaking up the drink. The cashier blinked up at us; her figure was barely visible beneath the uniform. She wore a green hat over her stringy, wet, blonde hair, with stray strands escaping around her flushed face. She was wringing her hands, sweating.

"H-hi," she murmured, her voice sinking beneath the hum of refrigerators. I rested my fingers on the resin-wet counter, tapping them impatiently. The wood felt swollen under my touch The cashier shifted, fidgeting with the hem of her green station jacket. Flynt remained cemented to the dirt-speckled tile. His eyes briefly met the cashier's—glassy, detached—and then moved on.

"Uh—hey, let's go. Fuckin' scan it. Shit's not that hard," I said.

Sweat trickled down the cashier's temple, freezing against her skin, her half-hearted smile revealing jagged teeth. Her name tag caught the weak light, its golden sheen glaring against the green fabric of her uniform; both were tidy and clean. Its surface read *Braelyn*.

"Y-yeah," the cashier stammered, wiping her brow with the back of her hand, leaving a streak of moisture. Braelyn chuckled, the sound faltering in the station, her gaze darting between us before she glanced down at her feet. Beside her name tag was an orange pin, an emblem of five intersecting suns.

Braelyn fumbled with the bag and drink, her hands shaking as she strained to reach for the scanner beside the register. She scanned the drink, the deep purple sliver of light flickering against the surface.

"Uh, what…what brings you two here?" she asked, her voice unsteady as she scanned the bag, her sweat slicking across it. My fingers brushed the cool, sticky counter as I slipped my hand into my coat pocket, brushing against cold metal. I dropped my gaze to her trembling hands, where the bag brushed against the edge of the scanner.

"Food. What's it look like?" I glanced toward the front window. Orange neon fuzz clung to the glass—letters warped in the glare: *Godfrey's*. It bled across the counter, bent in the steel rim of the door, and caught the floor in streaks.

Flynt shoved his hands into his pockets, staring thoughtlessly across the counter.

"Your total's…" Braelyn started, her voice trembling. The scanner beeped sluggishly. "Sixteen seventy-five."

A cacophony erupted behind Braelyn; metal shrieked, ripping through the peace. Shadows jittered across grime-caked surfaces as the light stuttered. A skinny silhouette slouched at the back, motionless in the squalor. Pots and pans crashed to the linoleum, their sharp discord ringing hollow. Long, thin white cats hung limp from hooks along the kitchen walls.

A tall, pale woman emerged, moving sharply, colliding into the counter. She put her arm around Braelyn, casting a shadow across the stiff grain lining the worktop. She stared across at me.

Pale skin pressed against the stark blue of her uniform. The woman's hair was jet-black, slicked back, glistening under the fluorescent lights. Her lips curved into a sharp, wide smile, white and prominent. She leaned into Braelyn like a drunk, her weight shuffling them both aside. Braelyn recoiled, staggering as the towering figure straightened up. I watched, hand hovering over the bag.

"Sorry about that," the woman said, her voice smooth as the surface of the counter. My fingers tightened, the edges digging into my palm. Tension coiled in my chest, breath catching.

Braelyn mumbled into her sleeve. As the taller woman leaned over her, I glanced at the five suns pin on her work jacket and the gold-tinted name tag across from it reading *Eleanor*. Eleanor smirked, unbothered, her presence like a chill creeping through the station's stale warmth. My gaze lingered on her for a moment longer before snapping away, focusing instead on the near-empty aisle, the dim light flickering overhead.

Eleanor's hand came down on Braelyn's with a decisive thump. The scanner slipped from Braelyn's grip, skittering across the counter before it smacked into the register. Braelyn flinched away, shoulders hunched as she twisted free—staring off at nothing, hands frozen at her sides.

"Right. Shut me out," Eleanor snapped. "That works beautifully."

My hand stopped, chips crinkling in my grip. Eleanor turned, the fluorescence sliding over her slicked hair. Her gaze pinned me, smug and steady. She shifted, her fingers brushing the hem of her crisp uniform. Her smile widened, slow and deliberate, fixed on me.

"There's no need to ring them up," she said, her tone smooth and absolute.

Braelyn flinched, her shoulders curling inward. "Uh—y-yeah, okay," she stammered, her hands shaking as she fumbled with the bag. The bag tipped, and her fingers scrambled to steady it.

Eleanor's gaze sharpened. "Freebies for you two darlings. A little gift," she said, the words carrying an air of something rehearsed but final.

"Cool." My arm dropped, the bag crinkling against my jacket as I turned away.

"Enjoy the moment," Eleanor said. Her smile widened as her voice lifted with a hint of sweetness. "You've returned to the scratch-and-lose, sugar." Her brows rose between the beat of her eyelids. Braelyn stiffened beside her, eyes flicking toward the door.

It's darker out there, isn't it?

I frowned, shifting my weight.

"Sure. Bye."

The lights stuttered—violent now—casting jagged shadows that slashed the walls. Shelves blurred at the edges, the corners swallowed by the dark. I stopped in front of the doors. Cold bled through the narrow gaps, a faint hiss trailing along the frame. It wrapped around me, prickling my skin.

I held open the door, the cold biting deeper as it seeped inside. My chest rose with a slow sigh, the breath faint against the gloom. I lingered on the tile. The door slipped from my fingers and shut with a muffled thud; the sound dulled as it fell into the dark.

I skulked toward Flynt, shuffling across the yellowed tilework. A chilling current stirred the air, ruffling my jacket against my ribs, coils rasping dry along my jaw.

"Flynt," I said, glancing back. "You done?"

His hand hovered near the drink on the counter. His gaze stayed locked past the attendants, blank and unblinking.

Eleanor's smile remained steady, but her eyes narrowed as she tilted her head. Braelyn's shoulders pulled tighter, her breaths uneven as her fingers pressed flat against the counter. Her gaze flicked between Flynt and Eleanor, her lips trembling like she wanted to say something.

"Run along now, Flynt darling. Go with Avery—be free." Eleanor turned to face the night. I tilted my head; my brows curled, nose wrinkled, jaw slipped slack.

"Hey. Uh…how do you know—"

The lights hiccupped—then died. Coolers along the walls hissed into silence. The black surged forward, choking the room. My grip on the chip bag tightened; its edge cut my palm, drawing a sting. The outlines of shelves dissolved, swallowed. Wind forced its way into the blackout.

CHAPTER 2:

I pivoted on a heel, turning back to the door. The tread scraped loose shards across fractured ceramic. My fingers wrapped around the door handle, the biting cold of the metal burrowing into my skin. Needles stabbed deeper, weight pierced into my grip, flesh tightening, taut against the chill. I flinched, but my grasp clung to the handle.

I leaned into the door, breath fogging the glass—shoved my weight into it, rattled the handle. But the door refused to open. The gas station swallowed the thud; dust trembled free from cracked walls. The horizon beyond the smeared pane—blurred and mangled—turned in slow, fluid coils. The parking lot was empty, lost in haze. Petrol pumps stood in rigid rows beneath a canopy of rust-eaten metal. Their outlines blurred within the darkness that swallowed the sky.

I jammed the crinkled bag of chips into my jacket pocket, the metallic rustle muted in the quiet gloom. I squared my shoulders, took a breath that turned to mist before my lips, and threw my weight against the door. Tendons pulled tight beneath my skin. My jaw locked, grinding with the force of it.

The door held still. I clawed at the seam, rammed the frame, then steadied myself. Fabric swished in soft, steady strokes as Flynt pushed off the counter. His sandals snapped across the tile, gliding past me with detached grace before stopping short of the broad, hollow pane that framed the lot.

He blinked. His palms pressed flat against the glass as he leaned forward, staring into the swallowing absence. There was a faint frost over the window where his breath touched the surface.

His gaze never wavered. I slumped once more against the door. A knot dug into my jaw, and my skin seized into the strain, breath coming out in short, white puffs.

My hand, pale against the door's dark glass, froze mid-push and pulled back. I tilted my head, catching Flynt's silhouette still and sharp against the window.

"Flynt," I said, my voice low, "I'm done. Come try this shit."

His lips barely moved—a low, half-formed gurgle—his eyes never leaving the blindness beyond the glass.

Eleanor slammed her forehead against the counter. The tip jar slid into a bowl of mints, rattling loose change against the glass. Lottery tickets scattered across warped takeout menus stained with watermarks. The whole thing lurched—coins jumped and spun before dropping with faint clicks. A crumpled map scraped over the tacky surface, snagged, then plopped into the tilted candy display.

A crash erupted from the kitchen—metal clattering, a tray slamming hard against the floor. The clang died, swallowed by the hush of water trickling over grit-speckled tile. Eleanor's smile didn't waver, but her head snapped toward the impact before she turned back.

Her fingers spread across the counter, nails dragging over sticky wood. Water dripped from the ceiling, splattering into resin streaks across the surface. She straightened with a sharp inhale, her elbows flaring, shoulders bunched, muscles biting.

Her hands tore at her scalp, nails scraping through greasy strands, yanking her hair away from her face. "Deadline's down the drain. Shouldn't I be working?" A brittle laugh broke free, thin and jagged, cutting through the air.

Her hands dropped, smoothing the damp fabric of her uniform with quick, nervous swipes. She grabbed a crumpled pack of cigarettes off the counter, shook one loose, and pinched it between her lips. The lighter came from her back pocket—flicked once, then again, flame catching on the third try. She lit the tip and drew in deep.

The glow blinked alive—small and mean. Orange flared, caught the edge of her cheekbone, flashed over the ridges of her knuckles. Smoke curled toward the ceiling, brushing the dark like a slow-burn fuse. Behind the counter, Braelyn's face showed faintly in the flare, pale and tight, eyes wide in the flicker. Shelves, pumps, and puddles beyond the glass stayed drowned in blackout. The flame hovered between them—a firefly.

"I—um. Maybe we should—" Braelyn's voice cracked, faint and shaking, like a thread about to snap.

Eleanor spun, lips stiff, teeth peeking through. "What? Use your words." Her voice broke the plink of dripping water. She leaned forward, eyes pinned to Braelyn's hair. "Go ahead, dear."

Braelyn shrank back, her fingers knotting the hem of her shirt. Her throat bobbed, words scraping out. "I—I thought maybe we could… check the breaker first." She toyed with her fingertips, head down, circling the nailbeds.

"Oh," Eleanor said, her voice thick and slow. She tilted her head toward the counter as water splashed into the puddle near Braelyn's feet. "You're probably right." She pinched the bridge of her nose, eyes shutting for a breath. Fingers tensed, then smoothed down the front of her uniform. Her shoulders dropped; her breath thinned. "If it is merely the power, dove, then the breaker will suffice," she said. "But if it is the eternal recurrence"— her arms unfurled, curtains peeling back above her—"and if we remain topside when she arrives"—her arms swayed, then dropped, and she folded inward, voice dimming—"then we will vanish together, darling."

Eleanor bit down on the cigarette. It jerked between her teeth—soft crunch, steady grind—burn flaring against her lips. The glow pulsed orange across her chin in slow, flickering bursts.

"That said—the breaker box." She clawed at the register drawer, knuckles whitening as she braced her foot against the counter. "An indignity," she muttered, breath thin and jagged. "My poor starling deserves better." She yanked again. The drawer bent with a shriek.

Coins sprayed from it, bouncing off the counter and spinning wildly before clattering to the floor. Eleanor's fingers trembled, her nails digging into the damp, grimy wood. Her jaw tightened, muscles twitching as her lips pressed into a line.

Her breath shuddered as her fingers twitched. She dragged them through her hair, flattening the same damp strands against her skull.

"Right." The word slipped out, raw and brittle. Her breath curled faintly in the cold air, flaking as it left her lips. Her eyes flicked to the ceiling, jaw tightening as a faint clattering echoed through the walls. "He's finally put it out, hasn't he?" She fixed her gaze on Braelyn's shoulder. "The return."

Eleanor's blue uniform blurred past the aisles, aimed straight down my row. Her dress shoes struck the tile in sharp, deliberate beats, the sound hollow in the stagnant air. She stopped close, starch and sweat clinging to her. Her shadow blotted out the patches of uneven tile between us.

Her hand shot into her pocket. The stiff fabric rasped under her fingers before the keys scraped free. They jingled faintly in her grip, her lips parting.

"Move."

I shifted, arms clamped tight. My knuckles cracked loud and dry. "Yeah. Sure. Fucking—"

"Thank you, dear." She wedged herself between me and the door. A huff of smoke clouded my face, sour from Eleanor's lips. I scowled.

The key ground into the lock, the teeth catching with a gritty screech. Her fingers whitened against the brass, the vibration from the latch dragging up her arm, stiffening her shoulder. The teeth turned with a click. She wrapped her knuckles around the handle and eased her weight into it—the door wouldn't budge. Her lips twitched as the keys slipped, clattering onto the chipped tile. Her fingers trembled as they uncurled, nails scratching the glass. The grip froze mid-motion.

"You can't be fucking serious," I mumbled. Sweat bled through her uniform, the fabric glued to her back. "Uh—I need to go home."

Her breath came shallow and stuttered, short bursts fogging the glass in uneven streaks. Behind her, water rushed faintly through constricted pipes. Wind whistled soft against the window panes, the warped glass rattling faintly in its frame.

Her grip slipped from the handle, hand falling limp at her side. She straightened, smoothing the sharp creases of her uniform with unsteady hands. A dull sheen of sweat glistened along her hairline, and her lips stretched into a delicate smile.

"Right," her voice cracked. "Let's not make a spectacle of this." She smoothed her sleeves, gaze tipping toward the back. "It's safe now, sweetheart. The hall is clear, and so too is the breaker. Go on and be useful."

My gaze slipped past her to the gas pump platform outside. The night clung to every surface, shadows pooling, pulsing, drawing nearer. On the very edge of the cracked pavement, where the concrete bled into the consuming dark, he dangled on the precipice of the night.

It was just a distortion. But the hollow outline lingered—a lifeless, cold body. His curls clung to his head, flattened into matted rings.

It might have been beautiful. His face hung slack, drained of breath, pulled into the void beyond the glass. Somewhere above, a heart watched the boy—an enormous, crushing presence.

Braelyn dragged herself from behind the counter, shoulders knotted, her breath curling faint and shallow in the cold. Her uniform hung limp, its hem frayed and stiff with grime. Her shoes scraped over sticky tiles, snagging where resin oozed from the counter's edge and hardened in puddles of amber.

The hallway loomed, a pit swallowing the dim glow seeping from the door at its far end. Faint light clung to the edges, but the center was depthless.

Her waist dug into the counter's sharp lip, body shaking over shallow breaths. She scampered forward, throat tight as she slowed before the hall's mouth.

Tears streaked her face, thin at first, then pooling into a crawling stream. Sniffling cracked through her throat. Her hands clawed at her scalp, then scraped at her hairline, twisting strands until her skin flushed raw.

Eleanor whipped toward the wet slap of shredded soles dragging over the tiles—a slow, uneven beat. Her gaze softened, though her lips twitched tight. She drifted from the door, her rigid stance melting into a loose, swaying posture.

"Oh, Braelyn," Eleanor said, her tone soft and syrupy, like she was soothing a skittish animal. "You wouldn't want to disappear, would you? Poor thing."

Braelyn flinched. "I—I'll check," she stammered. "But you said you'd come."

"Don't look so pathetic," Eleanor cooed, her steps deliberate. "I'm right behind you. The breaker's waiting for you, sweetheart."

Braelyn staggered closer, her steps wobbling. Her elbow clipped a pen cup, toppling it. They clicked and spun across the cracked black-and-white tiles. She flinched, twisting as her shoe skidded on one. Receipts burst into the air with her stumble, drifting down to stick against the resin-streaked floor and candy wrappers.

"I'm sorry. I didn't mean to make it weird, and I know I—I really should stop being like this." Her voice thinned. "I just ruin everything."

Her fingers scraped the counter's cracked edge, nails catching on the swollen wood. Moisture bled through, tacky against her skin, slick beneath her fingers, leaving a film. Her palm slid off, leaving her skin sticky. She wiped it on her thigh, streaking grime into the fabric, snagging on her fingers. Her breath caught, shallow and ragged, as she glanced back. Her eyes were flickering, glassy.

Braelyn froze. Her gaze dropped, thumbs twisting together. Tears slipped down her cheeks again, sinking down her shoulders.

"Oh, darling—what's happened?"

Braelyn's tears fell harder, streaking her neck. Her voice cracked, words splintering under the weight of her sobs. "I—I don't... I just—Flynt, and then bleeding, and—" Her hands shook. "What if it's worse?" She trailed off, eyes wet. Her voice split, low and scratchy. "I don't want to be a part of this." Her chest hitched. Her fingers balled against her ribs, then pressed in. "Why—why do I keep asking? Why do I even think this return could be better?" She clenched her eyes shut. "This one's already ruined. Just—" Her breaths surged and pulled back—a shallow flood, returning faster. "Just let me give up. Please?"

"Hey..." My tongue dragged across the backs of my teeth. "I have no idea what the fuck you're saying." I raised an eyebrow, slow and crooked. "But, uh…maybe next time will be way worse than you're thinking. That would be pretty fucking funny."

The room held still, then clicked shut. Braelyn's eyes sank. Her knees buckled. She swayed, caught between collapse and momentum. Eleanor stepped forward with a slow, deliberate grace, hands outstretched.

"Oh, sweetheart, it's alright. Nothing bad will happen—not to anyone." Eleanor's tone coiled, honeyed but sharp, the edge buried beneath her steady breath. "Look, precious—no blood! He's thriving." She bowed low with a sweeping motion, one hand gesturing toward Flynt. "It won't be like before. The return has given us yet another wonderful opportunity—a life to relive—don't you think?"

Braelyn sniffled, shoulders tight. "I—I guess—" The words collapsed into a shaky breath. She sniffled, wiped her nose, and nodded. "Yeah!"

Eleanor guided her gently—one hand at Braelyn's back, the other flicking ash as they moved. They stepped into the back hallway. Darkness swallowed the walls ahead; Eleanor's cigarette flared, stuttering light across the mold-streaked corridor as she herded her forward.

The back hall bled into blackness, walls blurring, but their shapes stayed—silhouettes flickered, sharp-edged, wire strung from above. In the hallway, they were lean and fragile, sketched with trembling lines.

I staggered toward the front door, crunching through loose, soppy paper—crushed a can flat beneath my boot. I planted my heel, took a deep breath, and hurled it forward. My steel toe ricocheted off the glass; pain jolted up the nail. I keeled over, breath locked, then jerked upright, off-balance, glaring at the door.

"If Godfrey's so sure that the door should have stayed shut," Eleanor's voice echoed down the back hall, her voice thread-thin, "it was never going to open anyhow." Her teeth bared into a grin she carved into the dark. "Braelyn," she said, lips peeled back in a smirk of cracked porcelain. "The return's gone out."

Braelyn's grip jittered, her knuckles white against cracked plaster. "I—I knew it. It's been out, then, hasn't it?" Her shoulders trembled. Braelyn stalled, then shuffled forward. Her fingers twisted toward the door, and the knob rattled in her grip, hollow. Nothing moved—nothing turned. It never did.

"Oh, sweet thing. Think harder."

"W-well, I—I wanna try the breaker. Just in case. I mean—m-maybe Godfrey hasn't done it yet." She pressed her back to the shadowed wall—arms crossed tight, sleeves yanked down past her wrists. "I just—I don't wanna be the first person she sees."

They stopped, then shifted along the wall. There was another door on the side of the hall. Braelyn hovered, shaking as Eleanor bobbed her head.

The side door groaned open; the sound slammed through the dark—the edges scraped against the frame. Fingers raked the shelves in uneven drags. Then a clack—a breath—a whimper. Sneakers scuffed across the room at the back of the hall.

The metal whispered—thin and static-laced, full of loss. Something moaned from behind the hollow steel. It choked out muffled, whiny and thin.

"Do you still hear him, dear?"

"S-sometimes I—I pretend—" Braelyn's voice broke, choking on spit, tears catching in her throat. "Pretend I don't."

A breath dredged up, then snapped.

"Don't fumble so much—it's embarrassing," Eleanor said with a soft laugh. "You must know, Godfrey already believes us to be helpless."

I glanced back. Flynt stood rooted by the front window; his arms hung limp, fingers slack by his sides. Frost clung in thin patches to his face, etched along the curve of his jaw, spreading over the loose folds of his beige garments. The fabric hung in a single, unbroken sheet, billowing, sterile, glazed with a faint sheen of ice. His skin, his breath—still.

The dark ballooned against the glass, thick and straining, the pane bowing under the pressure. I stretched—off-kilter—reaching past the doorway, flicking my hand in front of his face. He still didn't blink.

Mechanical feedback shrieked overhead—piercing. I jerked toward the comm beside the counter, its grill buried in the dark. The hallway's cigarette-glow barely reached, bleeding pale across the aisles.

"Sure! You can spend the night, Avery." The voice wavered—soft, its edges sagging on the breath.

I glanced around the station. The meat on the shelf jiggled, veins throbbing beneath its surface. Maggots penetrated the meat from the inside, twisting into delicate white moths as the flesh expanded. They emerged from the rotting tissue like fluid, their wings wet and sticky, flapping desperately off the surface.

A faint breeze nudged along the side of the station. The walls groaned, the foundation settling with a soft, brittle sigh.

The meat sagged, collapsing into itself as more moths peeled free, their fragile bodies translucent, veins in faint, cracked glass. They lifted in a stream, a perfect arc, spiraling toward the back hallway—silent, seamless. The swarm slipped through the mesh elevator door, wings slipping between the weave, vanishing into the dark. Stillness punctured the air. The slab of meat was gone.

A deep metallic grind shivered through the space, followed by a cascade of sharp, staggered clicks. Nothing changed. The dark stayed thick, untouched, swallowing the scrape as it fell.

Footsteps broke the still—Eleanor seized the closet door and slammed it shut. Braelyn trailed after, clutching the back of Eleanor's shirt as Eleanor smoothed her uniform with precise, clipped strokes over the stiff fabric. Her eyes darkened—hollowed out; her shoulders slumped.

Eleanor drifted up to the doorway and pressed her palm flat to the wooden trim, head cocked—fingers spread, delicate. "Flynt,

Avery—our precious breaker's gone and died. Godfrey left it outside with the return." She leaned in, eyes narrowed perversely; her breath curled into the pitch. "You're trapped, sweet things. Please do adjust accordingly."

Her footsteps stuttered—every other step, a quick jerk of her head. She drifted sideways, close to the elevator cage. Her shoulder clipped the mesh, and she snapped back.

"Darling," Eleanor whispered, her voice slipping into the stillness.

Braelyn's eyes flicked toward the dark, then down. "It's n-not Yamagzhal—it's not her yet—but…" Her hands twisted in the hem of her shirt. "Sh-she's closer than last time."

Eleanor stepped past her toward the front window. "She won't touch you. He'll handle it." Her reflection flickered in the glass—sharp and long—then she turned back, cigarette twitching between her teeth. "He's always on time, darling—punctual, if nothing else."

"But—" Braelyn flinched, nodding fast. "W-we're late. He won't—Godfrey won't open the door if we're too late."

"He won't open it at all," Eleanor said. "Dear, that door will never open for those who are used-up."

Braelyn's hands fluttered, then pressed flat to her stomach. Her voice dropped. "I—I'm sorry. I'm disgusting. I know."

I crept past the shelves—slow steps, heel to toe—shuffling toward the back.

Eleanor bit down. The cigarette twitched—soft crunch, steady grind. The burn flared once across her jaw, then dimmed. Her chewing sped.

"But, wh-when she gets here—she won't want to see us if we're down there," Braelyn whispered. "Right?"

Eleanor traced her jaw with one knuckle, eyes lifting. Then she stepped in—past Braelyn's guard, cigarette glowing between their noses.

Braelyn tensed. Her fingers dug into her shirt. "I—I don't really…" She hunched. "I don't want anyone to see me right now."

I shifted closer—toward the dark at the end of the hall.

Eleanor tilted her head. "You're shivering, darling."

"I'm not—"

Eleanor's hand lifted—easy—toward Braelyn's back. Braelyn ducked out, breath snagged, as she bumped the narrow wall.

Eleanor sucked the cigarette through her teeth. The ember vanished down her throat as the station vanished into darkness.

Fabric ruffled down the hall—a lighter clicked twice. A flame caught. Smoke rose thin and slow. The glow traced her jaw—sharp, hollow—caught in her eyes. The rest stayed drowned.

I swept across the station, my footsteps dull against the tile, the dark swallowing the space between us. I slid between them. Eleanor's hands snapped back from the mesh, fingers twitching. Thin strands of skin peeled away, rugged and curling, exposing pale, bluish tissue slick with veins that bled faint streaks. She flashed an exaggerated grin and shoved her hands deep into her pockets.

I glanced toward the front of the station. Flynt stood motionless. A pale moth clung to his head, wings broad and powdery, settled like a flower blooming from his temple. Its limbs sifted through his hair—parting strands, stroking the scalp—before it leaned in and suckled at the skin.

My fingers curled around the crinkled bag in my pocket. I yanked it free, plastic rustling in the thick air. The bag tore with a violent rip—black muck erupted, splattering across my skin with the hiss of searing grease.

Flynt drifted into the void behind the counter, silent in his footsteps.

I recoiled, hand slick with the stuff, jaw clenched against the sting. Black droplets clung, thick and burning. I flicked my palm across my jacket, fizzy sludge flaring out in broken ribbons. The rest brushed thick, black streaks with the trail of my hand. My mouth twisted into a snarl.

"Fuck." My lips peeled back as I stared down at it. Braelyn dropped into a crouch, drawn to the mess.

"Can I–uh— Are you gonna finish those?"

"Fucking—no."

"Can I have them?"

My breath shivered. A grin touched my lips. "Uh…sure."

Braelyn dropped to her hands and knees beside me, fingers splayed against the slick tile. Without hesitation, she clawed at the mess, scooping up sludge-soaked chips, shoving them into her mouth. Crunching—wet, frantic. She slapped handfuls against her face, barely getting them past her lips, black ooze streaking down her chin, dripping onto her uniform.

She hunched low, shoulders drawn in, cheek pressed into the tiles. Her lips parted—mush slurped through blackened teeth. Oil-slicked fingers groped the bag, glistening tar smeared across her knuckles. It vanished down her throat.

Clotted black slop dribbled from her mouth, streaking her chin, soaking into her uniform. She dropped another handful into her mouth—crunch, gulp—ooze seeping over pale skin in sticky trails.

"Mm—thanks," she garbled, a clot sloughing off her tongue, spilling between her teeth, smearing her lips.

I stepped back, burnt plastic and salt clawing at my throat. She was breathless, like she'd been starving.

"So good," she gasped between bites, licking the mess from her fingers.

I backed up—my boots scraped—grinding, skidding.

"Yeah—don't thank me for that," I said. "Fucking…mess."

I flinched; a sharp crack split the air—glass shattering.

Braelyn squealed, crumbs spilling from her mouth, black smeared across her lips. Her hands shot up, covering her ears as she stumbled back.

My fingers twitched. A draft needled through the room, kicking up wrappers. It threaded the pores of my jacket.

Flynt stood by the jagged maw of the shattered window, dust spiraling in faint currents around him, slipping through the cracks, thin and weightless. A crumpled green umbrella hung from his grasp, its metal shaft twisted, mangled.

The shattered front window gaped wide open. Wind howled through the jagged frame, biting cold, rattling shards loose. Darkness rushed in with it, smothering the station, swallowing the aisles and counter in a lingering haze.

"Flynt! You fucking freak!" I snapped. "Fuck opening the door— that was a good fucking idea." A laugh tore out of me, high and nasal, scraping up my throat. Flynt's gaze fixed—bore straight into me. "Maybe—uh, just—warn me next time you pull that shit."

His eyes darted—left, right—as if snapping from a trance.

"A-Ah! My umbrella!" Braelyn stared, eyes vacant, slack-jawed, a thin rivulet of black drool seeping between her teeth, threading down her chin.

Flynt's fingers loosened. The umbrella clattered to the floor, its green skin bleached against the squalor.

We were statues, framed by the hollow bay, the night clawing past the broken glass. My fingers itched at my sides.

Flynt sniffed, the moment stretching—empty-handed, staring past us into the dark, as if something outside still held him.

Eleanor edged closer to Braelyn, their shoulders brushing. Braelyn's gaze stayed locked on the broken glass, trembling, shards catching faint trails of dust.

"What compelled you to do that?" Eleanor surged forward, arms flung high in sweeping arcs. "We had time—plenty of time to restart the return, to see Godfrey!" Her shoulders heaved; fabric snapped against her frame as she gestured at Flynt. She cast a hateful grin, eyes narrowed to slits. "Do you mean to kill yourselves? Do you mean to vanish?"

I smirked, flicking a lazy wave. "Yeah, uh—nice meeting you. Hey, thanks for the hospitality, or—uh—something."

I jogged a few steps to the window. Glass crunched underfoot, shards grinding loose, scattering into the dark. My grin pulled stiff as Flynt's silhouette loomed unnaturally bold against the deep-sprawling dark.

Braelyn had crumpled, shoulders hunched, her face buried in her hands, sobs pulling her inward. Eleanor's arm hooked around her, fingers splayed stiff against Braelyn's back, her gaze pinned on me.

CHAPTER 3:

I braced against the edge of the empty metal rim as I waded through. Shards broke free and skittered down my shoulder, crunching beneath my shoes. The night air bit into my skin, clinging to the sour musk inside. I paused; glass marked the sidewalk left and right—straight, broken, endless. Another crunch echoed my step. My fists clenched at my sides as I waded through the bleeding veil engulfing the gas station. It swelled, inching forward with labored breath. I couldn't see past the parking lot.

A neon sign flared to life inside—*Godfrey's* in bloated, bubbly letters. I snapped toward the window. The glass was intact, the lane blank. Flynt was gone. A dull orange glow seeped out, casting a sickly pallor over the empty interior. The light bled across the walk, spilling onto the blacktop.

Beyond it lay barren, a concrete cliff split by faded yellow lines, dotted with seeds. I walked; gravel crunched underfoot, scattering a cluster of casings, roaches across cracked asphalt.

Half of the gas platform peered out from the encroaching darkness like a lit stage; midnight swallowed the other side. White moths swarmed above the pumps, their huge, erratic wings flapping in twisted, frenetic cycles.

Something naked sat as tall as I stood, hunched against the wall of the stop. It quaked, pale flesh stretched tight over limbs wrecked beyond the shape that held them. Open wounds riddled its body, honeycombed straight through its face and torso, weeping thick black ooze that dribbled to the pavement with a hushed splat. The tears pooled in murky puddles. It had been there the entire time. I could have seen it. I should have.

Long, trembling fingers scooped up a squirming mess from its lap—a mass of baby ducks, dark and slick, forming from the fluid leaking from its pores. It crammed them into the holes dotting its chest, each one slipping loose and sliding back onto its hips, leaving streaks of oil across its swollen, gurgling belly.

The creature's arm stretched toward me, tendons glistening with an oily sheen, fingers creeping closer to my feet. It shivered, a spasm twisting its emaciated frame, dipping lower, inching forward in a slow, grotesque bow. A chill crept over me.

"What the fuck are you?"

A touch, feathery-light, against my ankle.

My leg drew back, and I kicked hard. Its head snapped sideways, caving like rotting fruit. The body crumpled onto the pavement. Black fluid burst from the split skull, splattering the concrete, pooling around my boots. The twitching stopped.

Mites spurted from the holes in its pitted skin, scattering through the swollen marrow. I stepped away. Beneath the corpse, the ducks squirmed, feathers ruffled and matted, bodies jerking and twisting against its stiff hide.

The swarm of specks crawled and writhed over one another, burying the ducklings, tearing them apart.

I stood rooted to the bloodstained sidewalk. The ringing in my ears sharpened to a high-pitched keen, a faint rustle along the gutters. My ribs locked. The ceiling bulged. Between the skies, a heartbeat formed— wet muscles wrapping, clogged arteries throbbing through the station.

One by one, the nuts lining the blacktop twitched. Milky foam pushed from fine slits along their shells—slow at first, then faster. Thin white steam curled as it lifted. From within the foam escaped a shrill, warbling cry.

White moths danced under the overhang, wings beating a frantic tattoo against the night. Their blurred bodies flicked on cartoonish grins packed with straight white teeth. The air filled with their giggling—relentless, soft. A cold draft puffed across my neck.

A moth peeled from the frenzy, wings winding a silent path toward me. It hovered just in front of my face—taller than my head, smirking, ogling—then darted back. My fists whitened at my sides. The edges of my vision fuzzed into a noose—grainy, pale. Their snickering was high-pitched and girlish.

Seeds cracked—wet, thick pops. From each casing, black vines shot up, slick with moisture. They twisted mid-air, convulsed once, then stiffened. Metal pushed through their shells—first as glints, then as peaches. The fruit bulged, split, spat out mesh trusses that locked into place as the vines writhed downward. The concrete swelled—deep and fungal. Moss thickened along the twisting lengths, meshing as they hardened. The vines coiled together, locking into a lattice. Beams braced outward. The tops spread into broad, flat triangles—thin metal plates, oil-slicked. Rust bloomed along the edges, creeping in flaking veins. In the center of each sign: one bold white Y.

One shot up beside me. Its edge caught my arm. My jacket and forearm split open together, unzipped in a single fissure. I staggered back. My hand clamped down over the wound. Steel roots punched from the sign's base, winding down into the concrete. It held there—silent, undulating.

Blood slipped hot and orange between my fingers—smooth, clean oil. It soaked into my sleeve, spilled down my wrist, pattered on the concrete. I clamped down with my other hand, tried to flex my fingers. They didn't move. The seeds beneath me quivered.

The moths whispered, "Dry." Staggered—off-time—one after another.

I lunged for the front doors, fingers scrabbling at the handles. The door clung to its frame. I yanked harder.

"Open, you dumb piece of shit."

Inside, the lights hummed steady—clean tile, full shelves. Flynt stood at the counter, arms folded. Braelyn laughed into her sleeve. Eleanor leaned in, elbow set, mouth slow and sweet.

My boots thudded against the concrete as I threw my body weight into it over and over. I gasped, fogging the glass with each heave. My palms slipped on the metal, the coolness, the sweat slicking my fist.

It rose through the mesh, reincarnated from the tar pool beneath the street. Limbs snapped from the vines. Skin sloughed in flakes. Joints locked, then popped. The torso scraped loose—riddled with holes, a ruptured fountain gushing smooth, black water from dozens of heads. The sludge poured from its ribs, hips, throat, smooth and bubbling.

It grew. The signs vanished behind its chest. Its head passed the roofline. It twitched once, then sniffled. It was a deep moan, a wet gurgle rising and dragging, caught in the holes that burbled air as if drowned.

Then the door shattered; the whole frame burst into gems of melded glass and steel. A cold gust shoved the twinkling of wind chimes through the open frame.

I stumbled through the frame. One foot caught on the lower hinge as the door-glass slit my shin. I buckled—collapsed onto both hands, knuckle-deep in the flood.

Tar sucked at my coat—splashed up in strings, hissed against my wrists. I braced, shoved forward, and slipped onto my back. My palm slapped the floor; the goo peeled with me as I scrambled upright. It stretched in strands, wrapped under my nails, smeared up my sleeves.

Something sour chewed through my tongue—waxy. A breath punched out of me. The air hung open, cold and still.

A black pool stretched wall to wall; fractured stars floated on its surface.

The muck poured down my thighs. My jeans smeared black. Blood welled fast—a hot orange stripe spilled from the rip in my forearm, threading into the black. It spiraled wide, curled into slick rings that spun and bled apart. The mix hissed against my nails. My hand clamped over the gash, pinned to the throb.

My spine pulled long, stiff, and slow as I straightened out. The station opened around me—gutted, soaked, split wide. The counter sagged beneath loose pills, crumpled bills, split wrappers. A thin stream poured from above—cut through the laminate, split the slab in two. Candy packs slumped in the runoff; syrup clung to swollen coins, pooling in the warped dip.

The coolers stood open. Racks torn out and dumped, bent metal piled on tile. Shelves cracked in half and leaned into the dark, goods sinking. Cold, oily, slow to part, the tide slapped my boots. Loose snacks and mush-soft cartons drifted through the cracks, their labels peeled in ribbons. Boxes slumped, heavy with soaked grain.

I staggered forward. A figure knelt in the black at the center of the store. She trembled. Guttural sobs cracked from her throat, loud, then low, dragging up through her chest. The jacket hung thick on her frame—black, smooth, soaked. A white rose bloomed along the back, stitched with clean, fine thread. Stiff curls clung to her shoulders, still and matted. Her arms hung limp, fingers grazing the surface of the sludge.

My hands rose to my lips, shaking, frost crusting my palms. My throat burned as I screamed into the station.

"Flynt! Braelyn! Uh—other bitch!" The words tore out ragged. I waited, ears ringing. The station fell silent.

My eyes settled on the front window. The glass stood whole. Empty, the sidewalk stretched wide alongside the barren lot. The moths were gone.

I drifted closer, boots bruising the surface, muck lapping softly around the soles.

She looked up—eyes white, tears streaking her cheeks.

Black stone curved around the station's interior—a cave grown from the walls. Columns splintered up from the flood, knotted with shards of shelving still clinging to the rock.

"Please… Please don't." Her words slurred. A cough rattled up from her chest. Fresh tears spilled over her chin, dropping into the black. They hit with a soft patter, swallowed fast. "I'm sorry."

The air shifted. Cold brushed my face. I rubbed at my forehead—black clung to my fingers, stung hot against the skin. "I still…I—I still love you." Her breath fogged, twisting in the cold. "Really… I didn't mean it!"

Behind her, the back door creaked open. Beyond it: flat, depthless black.

"Uh… Move?" I edged closer. My gaze flicked between her and the doorway. "No—wait. Why do you look just fucking like me?"

"I'll really quit this time, please!" The words left her in a hush, thin and strained.

I hovered between ruin and neglect, beside a toppled shelf slick with tar. Stars shimmered in the black, captured in the shallow blood of the station.

"Don't scare me like that," she pleaded. "Please .."

I stepped sideways, circling her toe-first, keeping distance. Sludge dragged at my soles. Cold air crept in from the open door behind her. It cut through the thick musk inside the station.

"Open the door!" her voice cracked, frayed at the edges. "Please let me in!"

My hand brushed my jacket. The fabric was colder than the air. Above, the stars flowed—slow arcs across a dull glow. I stared at her. Her eyes glistened, swollen with tears. She trembled. Her lips parted.

"I love you," she said, mumbling in a low, broken tone. Her body tensed. "Please! Please!" she screamed, snot running from her nose.

I paced around her, slipped, and caught myself. Her head twitched, lips pulled tight around the sob jammed in her throat. Her eyes screwed shut—still, her face turned toward me. I stopped and leaned against the counter. Drizzle tapped my shoulder.

She wailed—her palms struck her face, fingers raking across her cheeks. Her hair fell loose, shaking around her jaw as she tracked me. The motion drained out of her; her body stilled.

"I was just joking. I was being stupid, and—"

The sentence snagged on a sob. Her spine snapped upright. Her arms dropped limp at her sides. I looked from her to the door. The stars trickled down—bleeding into rain.

A lump of soaked cigarette butts bobbed in the black. It bumped my boot, broke apart, and sank.

The woman's body jerked. Her head dropped into her hands. She whimpered—high, breathless. Her shoulders twitched once, then seized hard. She fell forward; her elbow gave out. Her palm slapped the floor. Muffled cries poured through her fingers, choked and thick. She gagged, coughed, then screamed again—wet and sharp, broken halfway through.

Barcode-eyes flared behind the shelves—hundreds: white, thin-striped, and glassy.

Her whole body convulsed. Knees scraped back through the sludge. One hand slammed the tile. The other smeared across her face, dragging spit and tears and mucus across her cheek in one long shake. She didn't breathe between the sounds. Whimpers split through it, cracked high and helpless.

I twitched. My hand rose a little, then dropped back. My legs locked in place. Muscles tensed. Her hair clung to her mouth. Her chest heaved with another sob—low and rattling. I looked at the door. Cold air slipped through the gap. It pulled at my sleeves. She wailed again—louder this time. Her face smeared against the tile. Her fingers curled hard and shook. I looked back at her. Then at the door.

My muscles coiled, then sprung. I bolted past her. Black water splashed underfoot, slapped my jeans, streaked the walls. It hit hot and stuck, burning.

My boots skidded across slick chip bags. One popped beneath me. I slipped—half-running, half-falling—breath tearing loose in ragged bursts. My hip grazed the woman's jacket. I careened off hallway walls, palms slapping against the peeling paint. My ankles burned. Slush gnawed at my shin, peeled it raw through soaked denim. Ahead, the hallway narrowed. The back door lay cracked open.

I crashed into the back wall, shoulder first. My boots slammed into the corner. One hand hit the door hard—a sharp jolt of pain. The other latched around the knob.

The handle bit into my palm. Cold against scalded meat. My grip slipped; one hand was useless, twitching. The other held, trembling. I gasped. My chest bucked, throat scorched. Breath fogged the glass. Blood ran warm across my wrist.

The wailing cut off.

I turned, a slow pivot on the ball of my foot. The hallway stretched back toward the station.

The woman was gone. It towered over the station, upright, motionless. The black behind it bent where it met its frame. Holes marked its surface—small, smooth, irregular. Some wept. Some followed. The fluid clung to its body, ran in streams.

My breath caught. I clenched the doorknob tighter as I forced my gaze away. My foot crossed the threshold. I marched through. The door slammed behind me.

CHAPTER 4:

I stepped out onto white wood. The boards gave under my weight—dry, but soft. Wind chimes hung still from a crooked hook, silent in the draft.

Behind me, the wall faded from siding to pale brick, mortar black and dripping between the seams. Black leaked past the door, slick, slow, tracing a line down the first step. It slipped between the wooden railing and spilled onto the narrow path that cut across the dead yard. The trail had cracked, its edge peeling back from the porch where wood pressed against cement. At the far end, the concrete fused into broken asphalt.

The sky above lay flat—black on black; a stalker nestled against the edges of the station. I walked forward. My boot nudged the creeping fluid. It dragged with resistance, clung to the step, then resumed its slow descent.

A stale gust pushed through my hair. Cold slid through my sleeves, bit my ribs, scraped the backs of my legs. My fingers curled around my jacket zipper. I rubbed my arms. The metal stung through the fabric. I blinked hard—dry air burned my eyes. My lips cracked as I exhaled.

The porch swing creaked once in the wind.

A dumpster pressed tight against the dark, half-swallowed in shadow. It loomed—filthy blue steel, thick-ribbed and lidless, streaked with rust. On its front, stamped in mechanical black letters—clean, round, evenly spaced—it read *Balthazar*.

The bin sagged under its own weight. Trash bulged past the rim, stacked and rotting against the bricks. Bouquets of soggy cardboard sloughed from the pile. White skins split along plastic bags—stretched thin, peeled back, trembling. Fluid leaked in meaty ropes, glutted; it slicked the steel, crusted over in wet folds.

Pink scarabs hung above the sky on strands of floss—long, clear. They drifted in lazy circles. Ribbons of black mites surged from the folds, pulsed along the wrappers, curled beneath split cans. Then the scarabs lifted—reeled back into the dark in one smooth pull.

A generator crouched in front of the dumpster: blue rod-frame, paint flaked and eaten. At its center, a square black box; a wide funnel crowned the top. From the side, a cord slithered out, burrowed into the station wall.

A tongue spilled from the spout—long, gray, slick with moldy yellow spots. It coiled in fat, soft curves; the tip lapped at a shallow puddle. Along the mesh rods, cauliflower ears pushed through the frame— blue, swollen with yeast. They rose fast, crisping at the edges—burned through from the inside.

Flynt stood above it. His face hung slack. Eyes dull, drained out, he stared through me, then down toward the generator.

To my left, the front half of a short, rusted car jutted from shadow. The back lay buried in night. Headlights glared at the white brick wall, dim against stone. Wipers dragged dry across the glass—slow, squeaking. The frame was low and wide, the metal smooth and pocked with chipped blue paint. One back tire sagged flat. It straddled a yellow line, front wheels angled across two spots, crooked over a fading row of painted stripes.

The night moved around it, rose and fell against the concrete. Lapped against the trunk, then slipped back. The cabin choked, stuffed with shirts, trash, and crushed paper cups. A black ashtray on the dash smoked against the glass, staining it with thin trails of gray. The seat beside it held a pile of crusted clothes—sleeves bunched, collars stiff, pockets wide open.

Braelyn stood at the driver-side door, both hands on the handle, body pressed to the frame. She yanked it. Then again, arms trembling— sharp, erratic pulls. I clenched my fists. Blood slid down my forearm.

I stepped down from the porch. The stairs groaned under my boots—planks swollen, sponge-soft, edges dark with moisture. A wash of black sludge clung to the base of the steps—thin, sticky. It gripped my soles as I crossed the concrete.

Braelyn's fingers locked around the door handle, shoulders hunched. She yanked once, then planted a foot on the frame and hauled—elbows snapping back, whole body jerking. The handle rattled. Metal popped. She stayed pressed to the car, skin pale in the flicker of the headlights. I stepped forward—even footfalls—smears of gutter-paint drawn behind me in quiet strokes. Braelyn dropped her head against the glass and sniffled.

I stepped behind her. My hand clamped her shoulder. Her breath caught; a gasp punched from her chest. She turned, eyes wide and wet. She stared up, mouth slack, jaw trembling. I grabbed her by the collar of her uniform and yanked. Her hands scraped down the car's side as I pulled her back.

The wall caught her. Her head struck brick. Mortar flaked and stuck in her hair, dragged downward in a black smear. Her knees buckled. I shoved her upright, pinning her there. She shook. Her fingers hovered midair, twitching. Her mouth opened—useless.

"Where is that bitch?" My breath hit her face. "What the fuck did you do?" She flinched. A tear slipped from her left eye, broke on her cheekbone. Her mouth closed. Her chin dropped to her chest. I let go. My hand slipped into my jacket. Fingers brushed the lining. My eyes stayed on hers. "Why'd you go through my shit?" Her gaze wandered, then dropped. Her legs gave. She slid down the wall, uniform streaked with black. Her back hit the ground hard, elbows tucked in tight. Her face vanished behind both hands. She quivered beneath my hand. Blood tracked from my forearm, thick drops pattering onto the concrete.

Her chest rose fast, then stalled, then started again. Her lips trembled. A line of spit stretched between her teeth. The white spigot cracked against the bricks as her knee knocked it.

A sappy green hose hung from it—thick. It brushed her leg, slid down her ankle, left a smear. Then curled around her shoe like a fern, slumped limp, leaking.

"Hey." I leaned a forearm against the brick; my shadow eclipsed her face. Breath stirred her hair as my tongue flowed over my teeth. Braelyn stared past me. The heat slicked sweat across her skin. "What the fuck was that out there? What the fuck did you people do?" I nudged her with my shin. Her head jerked up. "You drug me?" My hands twitched. "Did you go through my shit? What did you take from me?"

Her face was slack; fingers trembled where they pressed the concrete. Her eyes swam. "Where's my—" My mouth locked open. I stepped back. "Where's my gun?"

It wasn't yours to begin with.

She turned her face away. Her face scrunched tight, chin shaking; tears welled, then leaked in fat, steady lines. They caught the glare of the headlights—cut down her cheeks, and vanished into her collar.

"I'm sorry," her voice cracked. "I'm sorry." It peeled off the wall in dry scraps and bled into the cold.

"It's dry."

I turned. Flynt stood in front of the generator. His silhouette filled the center—shoulders sloped, hands slack. The machine behind him was open.

Braelyn shifted. Her arms uncurled from her knees. Palms dragged across the concrete, smearing grit into thin gray streaks. Her head tilted toward me—eyes lifted—small, glassy, fixed.

I stepped toward the generator, my heel lifting slowly. Gum-thick puddles stretched beneath my boot; cold bled through the sole. Heat scrambled up my fingers, hands useless at my sides.

Flynt tapped the gauge. It clicked—small, hollow. The needle stuttered, then froze.

"Oh. I've got you. I got an idea." I faced Braelyn. Her eyes widened. She flinched, a high-pitched gasp punching from her throat.

I scratched the side of my head. My other hand slipped down my jacket, elbow dropping limp at my waistband. I stared into her face. Her hair clung to the mortar-slick wall behind her. Black streaks crusted at the ends. Her uniform was wrinkled, collar tugged low, fabric warped around the shoulder seams. She stared past me.

"Uh…could you get that for me?" I lifted one arm, slow. Pointed toward the spigot above her. The hose coiled beneath it, sagging against her leg. Orange blood trickled down from my finger, soaking into the concrete. My skin peeled from where it drained—wet tatters dangled along the back of my hand.

Braelyn's eyes darted to the puddles. Her breath stuttered behind her heart—tightness stacking in her chest.

"Oh!" She stiffened. Her spine scraped flat against the wall. Her knees bent.

She reached for the hose; metal hooked her finger as she twisted. Her hand trembled, the hose shaking with it. Her thumb slipped, then caught near the base. The hose came free. She looked down—lap soaked, mesh stuck to her palms, black and tacky.

Hands on the wall, she pushed herself upright. One foot slid out. She clenched the wall with both hands, face squinting tight.

My eyes dragged after her. Braelyn stood, straightened, met my eyes. Then she folded in again, eyes down. She held out the hose. Her arm shook; the rubber swayed from her grip. I took it and looked away.

Overhead, the black leaned in—soft-bellied, damp. It puckered against the sky's tongueless skin, licking at the roofline, the concrete, the backs of my legs. The black tide swelled at the edges of the station. It pooled at my boots.

The concrete flaked beneath my heel. Each step sheared off a thin crust; soft beneath, spongy. My boots scraped through frostbit grit. Blood had dried in a hard crust inside one nostril. My fingers stiffened at my sides, joints locked. The blood in them dripped, thick as syrup behind the skin. Pressure built behind the joints.

A hiccup caught in my throat mid-step. I swallowed against it. The windshield wipers scraped dry.

A new sheet of trash slid over the lip of the dumpster. Paper bags sagged there, dark and sticky. Knotted cables ran through the pile—wrapped tight around splintered foam, bent plastic, a torn sandal. Grease-stained wrappers hardened at the base. Receipt paper clung to the metal wall in bubbling strips, yellow and flaking. The back wall bowed inward, rust softened to pulp.

I stepped closer. Reached out. My fingers hit metal—cold, then tacky. A slick skin clung to the surface, layered over something sticky. It coated my palm.

I hauled myself up. Forearms folded over the rim. Knees braced against the side. My chin pressed into the crook of my jacket.

The garbage rose—slow, swollen, tight through the bags. I hiccuped. It hurt behind my ribs.

Black mites crawled through the pile, circling a white canister half-submerged in the center. A melted plastic handle clung to its side, tangled in a mess of dark hair. Crushed flat, a work glove held something pulpy. From a twisted strap, a rusted padlock dangled. A blackened bandage strip curled around the nozzle.

My arm sank into the heap. The trash funneled around it—sticky, waxy—clamped my wrist. I closed my fingers around the canister. I yanked, and it rang with a wet pop. Hair stretched back in long, slick strands.

Sludge smeared my sleeve. Clumps of gray paste clung to the elbow. Cracked sticker fragments stuck to the cuff. A pale, wet receipt pasted itself across my forearm.

I hiccuped. Mites scurried over the fabric. One by one, I peeled them from the sleeve and snapped them into the dark.

I scraped the canister down my leg. A wad of white fur stuck to the edge. A shredded rubber thread hung off the handle. The glove's contents had soaked into the corner seam—dense, pink, and soaking wet.

It hung from my hand, dripping down my jeans, as I turned away from the dumpster.

The air bit at my skin. I moved toward the car—its blue dulled to near black, pitted and scraped from hood to trunk. Scratches wove lines through the paint, some nail-deep. Rust bled from the edges. The door handle scraped ice from my palm when I touched it. I popped the fuel latch. The metal hissed against my skin—dry ice against my palm.

I hiccuped—the headache was back. I knelt. Gravel dug into my jeans. The hose was stiff. The fuel cap clinked off the body as I shoved it in. I leaned closer. The patterns blurred beyond star-shaped rims.

Inside, the ashtray overflowed—filters yellowed, packed tight. A crumpled pack lay open on the passenger seat. One cigarette left, crushed beneath the lid. The inside of the glass was brown.

My hand hovered near the door. I blinked. "No—no, I had it." The words slipped out, soft. I stared at the handle. "I didn't fucking leave it…" The wipers started again—slow, dry, scraping. A low pressure built behind my ears. Something in it ticked. Rubber scraped the glass. A heartbeat kept steady, deep. "Why would he even fucking take it?"

I wrapped my lips around the hose. Oil and rubber pressed to my tongue. I sucked. Gasoline fumes scalded the back of my throat. I spat onto the pavement. The white plastic canister slipped in my grip as I slid the hose down. My hands locked around it, but the pressure was weak. I scraped fuel along the rim.

I hiccuped. Gasoline fumes climbed around my face. My jacket caught droplets along the sleeve. I crouched there and stared at the car's flank. Rust gathered in strips. Frost pulled itself tight along the lower edge of the window. The cold burrowed inside—past the wrist, past the elbow. My fingers scraped paint off the fender.

"Please…" The wipers stopped. Behind me, Flynt coughed into his sleeve. I stood into the torrent of gloom that spattered the car. "Please be okay when I get back."

The air peeled the skin from my lips. Corners of my mouth cracked. I flexed my jaw; the joint froze mid-click. Skin split along my knuckles—fine, curling slits with frozen blood inside, dark orange, crusted with glassy frost.

I stepped forward. Something tore near my heel—brittle, sharp, like shedding bark. Pieces flaked off inside my boot.

My throat closed. Cold slush pooled at the base. My chest locked under the weight—breath came shallow, clicking against my ribs.

My fingers fused to the plastic canister. I pried them loose, peeled them like stickers. The last one ripped free with a wet snap. A layer of skin tore upward in a strip—meaty, trembling.

The sky pressed lower. Black rolled over the station, climbing the walls—white bricks, seams of black mortar, drenched. There was nothing beyond that. It folded inward, swallowing the lot behind the dumpster.

The darkness thickened behind Flynt. He stood at the edge, jaw slack, eyes wide and fixed above the dumpster. He stared.

It bled from above—silk in water, folded through the air, leaked between bricks. Her hair dragged it down in slow waves.

It crawled, oozing into the cracks between sound and movement.

"Flynt." It came out dry. "I'm, uh—I'm going home…to check something."

I stepped forward. The canister thumped against my shin. Fuel sloshed inside—sluggish. One hand still clamped the handle. I stumbled toward him.

Then the night exhaled.

A force uncoiled from behind the bricks, slow and rancid. Returned from the foot of the stairs, it became swollen with memory.

Yamagzhal rose past the roofline. The sky bent around her, dipped toward her center. Midnight clung to her ribcage—cooking oil pouring in glossy threads. Arms stretched straight up, past the canopy of night. Joint after joint, knots at every turn, curves and hinges. Wet roots joined her fingers—pale, soft, boneless at the tips.

Her skin was colorless—bleached flat. Pores looped across her body—smooth tunnels slick with black, veined in silver. Inside, oil caked thick over water.

Her sweater hung limp off her shoulders, pale pink, dotted with faint gray spots. The fuzz had hardened, thick and wiry, burned tufts of steel wool. The same holes had melted through the fabric.

Her arms jerked—rolling in slow, smooth arcs above the station, wrists folding, fingers spiraling wheels.

Stamped flush to her head—a ceramic plate, pale and dull, light deadened across its surface. Two tall rabbit-ears jutted straight up, flat and thick; blunt at the base, clean and rounded at the top. The eyes opened wide, ovals scratched over and over, looping scribbles packed dense across the upper half. A triangle sat centered below—sharp-angled, black, the same heavy scrawl dragged tight through the middle. The mouth pressed low, etched in a curved split: a hard crease at the center, twin arcs hooked outward. The ink writhed as she moved.

Hair poured from the base of the mask, pin-straight. It streamed past her waist, across the pavement, slick with runoff. The fog of midnight pooled beneath it, spreading outward with the strands.

Mites rippled in waves across the hair—stars falling through her braids. White moths clung to the constellation, etched against the strands. They drowned in it, folding deep, flapping slowly as they sank.

The heartbeat had returned. Her rhythm pulsed—folded the sky into a needle. The cold clenched tighter at the heart.

She had been there the entire time. I could have seen her: Yamagzhal—the law of eternal return—the tide gagging on a new carcass.

Braelyn's chin snapped up—fast, sharp, her head tilting like a struck bird. Her hands shot toward her face, then froze mid-rise; fingers splayed, held stiff, just shy of skin.

Her pupils clenched—tight, circular, sudden—they shook. A gasp punched free, wet and high, broken at the edge. Her throat jumped. Skin jerked beneath her jaw. One hand scraped at it.

Her gaze climbed, paused, twitched sideways, climbed again. Her neck hitched, and her head kept lifting, then stuttered in place—eyes dragging, pulled into the return.

Her feet scraped backward. One heel caught on the asphalt; her legs crossed at the knee. She twisted and dropped sideways onto the pavement. She let out a chirp as her hip smacked the ground.

Her earring caught the seam of her uniform. The chain tensed—then tore through her earlobe.

The green star flipped through the air and spun across the asphalt. Blood trickled after it—thick, black.

Braelyn's chest jumped. Her breaths were shallow. She dropped to her side and scrambled forward, hands dragging through the grit—skin rasping over fractured concrete, catching on flecks of glass. Her knees knocked together as she scuttled closer to Yamagzhal, palms sweeping fast across the filth. One hand smacked metal. She lurched, slammed her fingers down, and closed around the earring. Her grip trembled. The chain was slick with blood.

Her hand shook, pressed close to her chest, fingers clutching the earring tight, the sharp star-points slicing into her skin. Blood slicked the metal, streaked her knuckles. Her other hand hovered at her ear, twitching over the torn flesh. Black tears carved paths through the grit on her cheeks. Oil threaded down her neck in thin, sticky rivulets. Her eyes stayed wide—wet, unblinking—fixed on the dark cavity where Yamagzhal simmered.

Flynt stood lopsided, arms loose, head craned toward the sky. His chest caved inward. He stared through the mask into the churn. Black poured down into his pupils, burned against the surface of his eyes, held there like soot caught in glass.

I dropped. My knees slammed the concrete; palms struck, skin bursting across the seams. Cold knifed through. My fingers wrenched backward, crumpled past the joints. A nail dragged; it split open. Acid-eaten skin stretched thin, crusted in frost. Blood threaded the fractures.

My throat cinched; muscle cords twisted in on themselves, slick and shaking. Something swelled from my gut—wet, stinging—forced up the center, packed behind the sternum. The pressure kept rising. The next breath hit closed meat as it heaved.

Cold air festered behind my tongue; gums peeled from the roots—loose, sour, pulsing—burning in sweet saliva.

Yamagzhal boiled, her teeth trapped beneath the slab. The concrete ran cold in waves; each impulse lapped out from inside of her. It slid under my ribs and pulled at the joints. A stack of plates clicked beneath the concrete.

The heart of Yamagzhal bubbled up from the gutters. "Keep it pouring. There's nothing like buttermilk pancakes," it said. The voice was thick and phlegmy. A griddle hissed; the faint thump of a mug placed carefully—syrup peeled from the laminate.

"All that, and I'm still hungry." A bubble popped in a milkshake; vinyl shifted under the booth seat.

"Butter don't run like that unless it's right," whispered in a high, breathy rasp. Toast cracked; a deep swallow—ketchup squelched, fries rustled.

I shoved against the concrete; skin tore from the heel of my palm in a long strip, flayed clean to the forearm—the joint split, pushed out, surfacing bone. Dirt clung inside the tear; black grit webbed through the flesh.

Flynt advanced—steps spaced even. His chin tilted up, gaze fixed where the sky pulsed black, pressed low and breathing.

Sandals pressed through gristle, bottle shards, rotted foam, a tangle of hair sunk into bile; dragged filth in strands behind him. His arms hung loose, spine held taut beneath it.

The dark met his shoulder—it slurped and gulped.

Yamagzhal's outline held human: her skin was milk-glass draped in wet linen, tiled in man-framed doors cut from rose quartz. They rippled across her body in gentle waves. Behind the glass, men flared and vanished—returned to her.

He stepped again. The tide crashed over his chest.

A swell hit behind my heart. Oil heaved through the centerline; it scalded the throat, dragged bile, spilled over the tongue. I gagged, bent, vomited black across the concrete. It splattered against packed stone—steam peeled up, thick, sulfur-heavy. Another convulsion tore through me; orange bled through the slick.

My elbows locked; pressure popped through the joints. I shifted forward, dragging a knee beneath me—skin tore across the cap. The other bent with it; tendon slipped, caught, burned. Wrists pressed into the stone, bones grinding tight. I drew my hips up. My back arched; knees buckled under the weight. I rose—shoulders first, then back, then head—breath rasping through clenched teeth.

The generator flared. Fog pulsed around it—slow at first, then faster, folding inward. The light bent. Its edges slipped; shape split and realigned; planes turned inside-out. It tilted sideways—then forward—then again.

I shoved forward—breath hot in my mouth, plastic clanging off my hip—weight bucked sideways. My boot landed nowhere; my grip tore loose; the canister twisted, yanked, vanished. Then—tilt—drop.

Palms hit gravel, skinned clean. My knees cracked down next, folding hard—hips turning—shoulder grinding. I turned with the fall, rolled once, then staggered half-up; the floor dipped beneath me, rising again, pitching sideways as the dark breathed slow against my ribs. I braced—one leg bent, foot sinking into honeycombed concrete—hands scrabbling slick with orange. Flynt was gone. Braelyn was gone.

The dark crumpled—depth slipping out of line. My step landed off-axis; the boot scraped something flat that dropped away mid-stride. Weight pitched sideways through my hips, twisted through my ankles. I lurched—caught the generator with both palms. Metal bit into them. I pulled back; skin tore loose.

I fumbled with the cap. Cracks split through my fingers as they slipped along the ridges, blood mixing with oil, nails scraping, feeble, until I dropped my shoulder into the thing and twisted. The metal groaned. My wrist snapped sideways. The cap broke loose.

A second tongue flopped free from the generator's spout—white, bloated, veined. It fell onto the black one, twisted in, coiled tight. Together they flexed into a rope; the tip licked my laces.

I shoved the canister forward. Its mouth met the socket, locked in place. The liquid gurgled low—echoed hollow, then damp. Something sloshed behind it.

Oil spit up along the rim, speckled my knuckles. My hand stuck where it held—skin blistered to the plastic. I peeled each finger back. The canister clunked off the casing, dropped to the concrete, and collapsed flat—splashed out in a milky puddle.

I mashed the cap down. The tongues squirmed beneath it; they coiled against the edge, then jerked back.

I scraped along the generator's side, hand catching on a bolt, fingers twitching dumb against the panel until the switch clicked under my thumb.

The generator hiccupped—once—then caught. Lights along its frame twitched blue and gold. A dry whine churned through the casing. The ears withered where they hung, flaked down to nothing. The tongues sagged from the rim, steaming; they slid loose, dissolved.

Light gathered under the back door, pale and growing. It pressed out across the white porch—poking into the dark. Above the steps, the wind chimes stirred—a cold bloom, thin and rising.

Yamagzhal leaned. Her torso folded in stages—hips hinged, neck held stiff. The mask strayed forward; its mouth jittered, then smoothed. From her shoulders, the arms dropped—straight down, then out; chalk-thin saplings reached over the lip of the dumpster. Joints split into roots—creased, dented. Bark-skin tore through damp fiber strands, clotted in the drift of trash-heat.

The dumpster groaned. Plastic warped inward—sheets collapsing, liners punched flat by the weight above. Metal along the rim sank in stages; the frame settled sideways; two screws popped from the back corner and spun out into the alley. Inside, curled bodies packed the heat-rotted cavity—naked, pale, hair sprouting in curls along their crowns. They clung in bird-heaps, their skin pressed together in soft, wet layers. Heads hung open. A wide hole sank into each from above—edges frayed and brown, centers gone to pulp. Limbs tangled and looped back; arms threaded into legs, torsos latched hip to hip. They hung from the branches in droves, limp. Toes caught. Necks bent backward, leaking blue into the trash-bed. One trailed from a tangle by its foot, ribs caught on a coil of bone. The gap in its head drained slowly.

Yamagzhal dragged the boy across the rim—held him under the mask. The body sagged from her fingers, ribs shifting around her. Blue ran from the open hole in his head, dripping into the bin. The mask lifted. Ceramic tilted with a dry click—beneath it, the second face pulsed wet-pink. A thick vein twitched down the center, sealed shut. The faceplate staggered into squares—pixel-spread, a low-resolution smear from top to bottom—then flat again.

When he neared the seam, his body sheared. Skin stretched long, then pinched to thread; the pressure crushed inward, silent. Hair caught on the rim and tore loose in ropes. Her fingers fed them one after another—soft at the joints, limp at the neck. They compressed fast—spines folded, hips snapped sideways, legs crumpled into the slot. The mask twitched with each pull. Thick black drool gathered beneath the rim.

Black sprayed from the seam, slapped the asphalt in globs. The puddles veined out in roots across the concrete. From the pools, ducklings hatched up through the goo, oil-slick and shivering. They waddled from the garbage water, their beaks hung open.

The slit clicked shut with a wooden knock. The branches retracted. Her hand dropped straight to her side. Blood caught thick on her palm.

I bolted across the lot. My boots hit uneven, shoulders listing, breath locked in my throat. The porch hunched ahead—white paint flaked, wet boards sagging under rot. My foot caught—wood cracked. I staggered, kicked loose a slat.

Yamagzhal murmured inside of me—her burden sank through my lungs.

I dug for my key, jammed it into the lock, threw the door open, and staggered through.

CHAPTER 5:

A single ceiling light burned above the back hallway—flat, smooth, yellow-white. Small black bugs crawled across the surface. The glow clung to the walls; the heat had curled the paint in patches, puckering around bulbs of blooming moisture.

Past the throat of the hall, the station ended. A slab of black met the tile, sealing the other side.

The hallway bowed outward, bloated with pressure. Swirls of green and blue paint bled from the seams where the ceiling met the wall—fanned out, then dried in ridged stains. The air pressed in, thin and humid.

Braelyn hunched forward—head pressed to the wall, arms pinned between her cheeks and shoulders. Her body shook; small, fast tremors. She sniffled. Snot crusted under her nose. Black clumps matted the back of her hair. Trails of the stuff streaked from ear to collar—thin, glossy ropes.

"Uh—how the shit did you get back inside already?" I asked, fixing my gaze on her earlobe. Blood trickled down the curve. She clutched the earring tighter—it sliced into her palm.

She gave the wall a soft thunk with her forehead—just once. "I—I can't believe you slammed the door on me." She sniffled. "You hate me that much? W-wow."

"Hey… Uh, I don't— Where's Flynt at?"

Two bathroom doors stood behind her, both crooked. The closer one gaped; the bottom edge hung blistered open, frame sagging around the hinge. The farther held shut—wood swollen, handle dark with grime. Across from them was the closet: a wide-open door, split down the center with wood-rot. Inside, the floor sank into a corridor—dim, narrow. At the far end, a grated, metal staircase spiraled down. Pipes curled along the ceiling; water plinked into a puddle at the center of the concrete, light stuttering across the surface.

Beside the closet stood the elevator cage. Its mesh tilted, one corner bent. Dust coated the bars—swirled loose into the enclosure.

My boots squished against the flooded tile—water rippled with each step.

The back wall stood tiled in paintings—dozens stacked edge to edge, layered and uneven. Each frame was the same: chipped, ornate gold.

A lighthouse recurred, rendered again in oil: thick brushwork, muddied sky, black ocean pulled flat across the canvas. But the perspective shifted. It was never the same.

Brilliant orange flared from the beacon—radiant across brush-slick skies. It pooled in the glass, but it couldn't reach the station. Still, the room felt brighter.

The bathroom door creaked open. Flynt slipped past it, shoulders bunched, hair wet at the tips.

"Avery."

He stopped in front of me. His shoulders drooped, fingers slack at his sides. His gaze drifted past my head, fixed on nothing.

"I wonder if you've changed." His voice came low—flat through the throat.

The black stud at his earlobe caught the light. His shirt sagged down the arms in soft, uneven folds; sleeves dangled past the knuckles.

One sandal edged forward. My jaw hung open, brows drawn in.

"Dude… What does that fucking mean?"

"Maybe that boy outside looks like your younger brother," he said. Flynt stood level—arms at his sides, fingers loose.

I slammed my hand flat against the laminate-paneled wall. "Fuck you. What the fuck is wrong with you? Don't—don't fucking bring up Gary like that."

I stepped back. Flynt's head tilted. His eyes flicked to the door beside us.

"Bathroom."

He turned and walked. His feet lifted delicately from the tile, peeled up with a soft rip. He snagged one of the tall lighthouse paintings off the wall, tilted it over his head, the canvas looming over his face as he eased toward the bathroom.

"Hey! Uh… Where are you going?"

The door creaked inward. He slipped inside; it dragged shut with a deep, uneven scrape.

"Motherfucker…" I stepped forward. Tile sucked at my boot. Water slicked the floor, slow and warm, pooled deep in the grout.

The hallway stretched before me—a narrow gullet. Metal groaned somewhere above.

My hand pressed against the cold steel of the elevator on the left. Rust flaked beneath my touch; orange dust smeared into the black fluid that stained my fingers. The mesh rattled under my weight.

I peered through it at the grated interior. The elevator reeked of disuse—a thick metallic tang that hit the back of my throat. Something dark had dried in the corner, bubbled and cracked. A smear ran down the rear wall. The lights above flickered once, then dimmed again.

I pulled back. Rust clung to my skin.

The light at the end of the hall snapped on—flat yellow, steady. The floor caught it first, then the walls.

Eleanor sat on a metal stool at the center of the beam.

Her back was straight. Hands rested in her lap, palms down. Strips of flesh hung from her fingers. Some nails were gone—raw beds exposed, skin peeled to the joint. Her uniform clung to her in soaked patches. Blood streaked her sleeves—orange, black, blue—dripping down her arms in gluey webs.

As it hit the tile, the fluid twisted. It rolled in the air, curled outward, fanned into petals. Roses formed on impact: wet, soft, and full.

Her face stayed still. Half her teeth were gone. The gaps showed when she breathed. Her eyes didn't track. Hair stuck to her forehead in ropes. A streak of color ran down the side of her throat—bright blue, still moving.

Behind her was a nest of corpses scattered across the tile—bent at sharp angles, stripped of skin in crisp, flaking planes. The bodies lay split clean down the center, their black jackets sliced at the shoulders. For the first time, they looked just like me.

Chests folded inward, halved like a shell; bellies torn into sharp-edged pieces, stacked inside themselves. Soft pulp knotted in the folds of fleece. One jacket still held the rose—stitched white on the side, half-soaked in black.

Their glass-white eyes hung open—slick, unblinking, buried in curls and blood. Faces turned at broken angles, jaws slack, mouths edged in black. Pale skin stretched tight over cheekbone and brow; some peeled back, stripped to the root, sockets rimmed in orange. They had the same nose, the same hair, the same face—jammed between shelves, cradled in the crooks of each other's arms.

Eleanor sat still. Her face slackened.

"I can't hear Godfrey anymore."

Braelyn trudged forward, feet dragging through the fluid. Her left knee buckled with each step. Her shoulders hunched, head low.

"Help…" The earring rocked between her fingers, streaked with blood. "Help. Help."

Eleanor turned. Blank eyes tracked the stumble.

"Well," she said. "You're here."

Braelyn inched forward, straight for the stool—eyes low, gait fractured. Her lips hung open, trembling at the edges.

"She's—She's already here, and—"

"I know," Eleanor said.

Eleanor tilted her head. Her hands rested in her lap, fingers splayed.

"H-how are we supposed to— What are we even— W-we can't? This isn't—"

Braelyn stopped at the base of the stool, wide, wet eyes locked on Eleanor's face. Sweat ran down her jaw. Her whole body quivered. Then the air left her in one hard sob. She clutched the earring tighter—its edge cut into her palm. She heaved forward and threw her arms around Eleanor, crashing into her.

The stool tipped. Eleanor rocked back with the impact, heels lifting. Her arms jerked up—held wide for a moment.

Braelyn sobbed harder. Her forehead pressed against Eleanor's collarbone. Blood smeared down the front of her shirt.

Eleanor steadied the stool. One hand landed on Braelyn's back. The other settled on her head. Her fingers moved slowly, tapping gently, rhythmically, as she stared forward into the hallway. Braelyn clung tighter.

"I-I d-didn't know what t-to do— He—he kept talking. I could hear him—and she—they were… It was—"

"I know," Eleanor said again. Braelyn's legs gave out more with each breath. Eleanor adjusted, arm tightening at her back to hold the weight steady.

"We'll see him together," Eleanor said. "It'll be alright."

Braelyn just shook. Eleanor blinked once. Her palm moved in slow circles against the back of Braelyn's head.

"B-but… Godfrey, he won't—" She choked on the words. "—even let us in."

"But, sweetheart, I know the way past his bedroom door. Once we reach the lower level, you will be safe."

Her lips slipped into a tender smile—brief, quiet. Braelyn stayed wrapped around Eleanor, face buried in her shoulder. Her hands stayed limp at her sides. Eleanor was still.

I stepped closer. Water shifted under my boots. The tide pulled.

"Uh—hey," I said. "What the fuck was that?"

No response. My voice was shaking. Braelyn's shoulders twitched. My eyes moved—wet floor, sick light, elevator shut tight, blood dripping down Eleanor's neck.

"Why was Yamagzhal out there?" my voice cracked. "How do I even know her fucking name?" Still nothing. Eleanor kept her head down, her mouth hung ajar. Braelyn clung tighter.

"I need…" I shifted my weight. My shirt stuck to my back.

"Can I just…go?" I asked. "Do you need me for this, or can I fuck off now?"

Eleanor blinked. Then she slowly lifted her head.

"No one's going home," she said. Her voice was low, quiet, and flat. She stared past me, into the middle distance.

Then she straightened. Her spine pulled long. Arms rose with quiet grace—elbows loose, wrists curled. Then her eyes lifted. Her voice followed.

"You'll be safer with him, dear," she said, smooth now—sweet. "He's waiting for you downstairs."

Her mouth twisted into a shaky grin. Her eyes fixed on mine.

"Godfrey," she recited. "He keeps you safe. That's all he's really doing." She turned her hands palm-up. Light flickered across her wrists.

"I need to go home… Just, please, let me check something."

"Sweetie—there's nothing else left for you to check."

Something swelled behind my eyes—hot, wet pressure. My vision smeared sideways; corners of shelves curved, then snapped back. I blinked a few times. Dry lashes scratched the edges; each blink carved the heat deeper. I pressed two fingers to the bridge of my nose—cartilage gave, soft and damp, under sweat-slick skin. Salty heat slicked my lips.

"What the fuck are you trying to say?" I twisted toward Eleanor; the veins in my neck throbbed hot against tendons and skin. "That my house is empty? That I fucking killed him? Fuck you." My head dipped. I smacked my lips—dry, bitter, the click stuck behind my teeth. "If I see Yamagzhal again… I'll empty the clip on that bitch. I don't care." My eyes burned.

Eleanor folded forward—bowed, shoulders crackling with strain. "Avery, precious, you've been here before. You have no home." Her words thinned to a rattle, drying up halfway through. "Even if you hadn't killed it," she said, "Godfrey would have."

I raked my hand down my face—skin caught against spit and grime with a Styrofoam rasp. Then I swayed side to side, tugging my jacket tight against my ribs. My gaze bore into Eleanor. "Well—uh—you're wrong. I have a home," I said. "I—uh—I need to go see my brother…" My head dipped, curls drooping forward, hanging over my mouth. "I think something's wrong…"

Her eyes narrowed—dry at the rims, crusted with orange and blue streaks. Light caught on the whites; her lip twitched.

"So…just…let me fucking go," I said. Heat burrowed behind my cheekbones. The pressure split into roots; they curled into the hollows of my brain, sucking and swelling into the soft tissue. Sweat crawled along my spine. My teeth ground together. "I'll fucking kill you, you know—just let me go!"

Eleanor smiled—a tender grin. She sighed, eyes rolling upward with the breath.

"Go ahead, ma'am." She drew a long breath, lifted her chin, and let her eyes drift upward—past the ceiling, past the rafters, into something darker. "I would love nothing more than to live this life once again. I owe the return so dearly for what it has given me." Her gaze stayed fixed above—fading. "But she's here now—the return is here: Yamagzhal—dying and rebirthing in a cycle of suicide. Soon, that will all be over with."

Then her shoulders sagged. The performance collapsed. Her arms dropped and swayed.

Braelyn caught her before the stool could tip. One hand gripped Eleanor's waist. The other steadied her chest.

Eleanor went limp. Her head lowered. Then her eyes dulled again—empty, unfocused, halfway shut. She shifted. Her arms twitched first, then her spine unwound, slow and strained. She peeled herself off the stool. Blood streaked the seat behind her, dark against the metal.

Braelyn stepped back. Her hands stayed open, hovering. Her face stayed wet. Tears kept falling, silent now, as she wiped them on her sleeve.

Eleanor didn't look at her. Her eyes held nothing. A flat line across her mouth curved just slightly—barely a smirk. She limped forward, left leg dragging behind the right.

She raised her head and glanced past Braelyn, at the torn edge of her earlobe. She tilted her head. Her grin went slack.

"What happened to your ear, sweetie?"

"What? Oh! I-it was my fault…" Braelyn mumbled.

"Don't say that. Do you want me to make you a new one?"

Braelyn held the earring tighter. Its thorns bit into her palm; blood slicked the star-shaped metal, running in thin lines between her fingers. Faint cuts bloomed across her hand—sharp and shallow, like paper-slits—where she pressed it hard to her chest.

"No! I mean—you already made me this one, and…" Braelyn twiddled her fingers.

Eleanor smiled. She glanced at Braelyn's hand and sighed—a long, warm breath through the nose. Her eyes softened, lips parting to bare a grin.

More blood leaked from her arms. Orange and black and blue and white. It ran down her sleeves, soaked into the folds of her uniform. The colors spread in sharp contours. The black and orange fell from her fingertips in thick drops that curled into rose petals as they hit the floor.

Her hand rose—shaky, fingers bent at the knuckle—and held down the elevator call-button. The doors stayed shut. The elevator didn't stir; the station remained silent, still.

The bathroom door creaked open instead. I turned to face the creak—leaned in.

The tiled floor stretched out—off-white, cracked. To the left: a shower, the curtain fallen in a soaked heap, rod tangled in the folds. To the right: a sink by the wall. The medicine cabinet above it hung open. Bottles littered the porcelain—some cracked, some emptied.

The tub was full. The water was running, overflowing onto the tile. Blood streaked the outer rim in thin, dry lines.

A window sat centered above the tub, high on the wall across from the door—its frame rotted, the pane cracked open. A soft breeze wafted through the space. My face went slack.

A speaker buried deep in the gas station crackled to life. Static rolled through in slow, steady waves—soft and wet, lapping surf against stone. Beneath it, a boy's voice mumbled, "Um—sure, Avery! Stay as long as you need…"

The white wooden door at the end of the hall creaked open. Deep-set grooves rippled across its surface—bitter and glossy, like pressed chocolate. The hinges strained. A crack of stale air slipped through.

Heat tore into the vents, stripped off my skin in sheets. The reflecting pool along the floor hissed at my ankles. It bubbled, then peeled back in greasy ropes that snapped across the soggy tile. Steam burst from the surface—roped into the vents. What didn't rise smeared backward across the floor, smoking as it dragged toward the back door, scumming the tile behind it.

Cold spilled through the room in waves—laced the vents, bloomed along the tiles, swallowed my boots. Steam pooled in my mouth. The tile whined underfoot. Frost etched through the grout lines—deep and splintering, cartilage swelling behind the walls.

The tiles peeled, grout cracking as they slid apart. They pulled away from each other and lengthened—stretched into slats of dull wood, pale, the grain damp with polish. Joints sat uneven where the boards met. Nails ran crooked along the seams, some sunk, some raised; the edges curled up at soft angles.

The walls split. From the plaster, black flowers bloomed—wet-petaled, fast-growing. They wound, peeled, then flattened into faded wallpaper. White trim grew underneath, grooved bark against the baseboards.

The bathroom signs dropped from the doors. Their metal clattered once before slipping through the cracks in the floor. The frames bowed and swelled into wood.

The lighthouse paintings warped. Glass split in fine webs as the paint bled—smearing, fading, turning silver-gray. The frames curved into mirrors, some round, some rectangular. A glare bolted once across the surface.

The elevator was still.

Yamagzhal stepped through the back door. Cold drowned the hall, its branches swelling out across the floorboards. The current drained the walls of warmth, snuffed us out in an instant.

Her breath churned in spirals—coarse and sharp, moist in the throat, rhythm thick and clotted. The wheeze echoed—low, steady, crawling through wallpaper and steel. Beneath her, the floor flexed in place—boards ticking inward, straining at the nail. The untangled room began to spool.

Her rabbit-ears tore the ceiling. Wires snapped from the drywall; pipes bent open, shedding rust and powder. The hallway twisted and caved as the mask scraped high. The ears carved deeper—a long drag across the plaster. She tilted her head. Chunks broke loose and fell.

Her sweatshirt bulged. Polka dots blinked and shifted over the surface. Her arms were wide and uneven, skin stretched into soft humps, discolored, half-dried. The fabric clung to her, twisted at the joints.

Her feet sank into the floorboards. The wood bent, split, and re-formed around her.

The mask was smooth, white, glued across the seams of the face. The eyes were ringed in a beading, flowing glaze, black lacquer. Light from the mirrors caught across its surface. My reflection in the return was pale and shattered.

Yamagzhal stood—winding. The ceiling overflowed. The pipes dilated; light fixtures pulled upward, cords drawn thin. Her ears passed through, then her shoulders. The hallway tilted to hold her.

Braelyn's face slackened: eyes wide, lips parted, unblinking. Eleanor stepped forward. Her boots clicked once on the warped floor.

Her hand shot out, grabbed Braelyn by the collar, and shoved her through the bathroom door. Braelyn hit the tile sideways. She looked back—mouth trembling, teeth bared, eyes wet and wide. Eleanor slammed the door.

She moved again—slower now, legs trembling. Roses unfurled under her steps—petals of pulp and bone. Her uniform clung to her frame; black, orange, and white bloomed across the fabric. She stepped through a tray of pulp. Her smile stretched, quivering at the edges of her lips.

She stopped in front of Yamagzhal. She looked up into the mask. Yamagzhal tilted. White ceramic—dull under the gas station fluorescents—reflected a crooked impression of Eleanor.

The mask turned—my reflection in the ceramic small, inverted, skewed. It dragged lower, tension pulling along her flaccid jaw. Then it slipped. A hollow thunk cracked off the tile—flat, dry in the frozen air.

Yamagzhal's face caved inward—flesh twisted into a black-and-white spiral, moist and puckered, folds layered into the ridges of a clenched throat. From its center, a thick gel squeezed out in pulses—dark, streaked with clots of pale scum. It dribbled in threads, sagging from the lip, then snapped loose. The strings hit the hardwood and stuck—drawing a tangled web across the floor.

Yamagzhal swayed—slow, off-tempo, joints straggling the bulk of her mass. She filled the hallway, floor to ceiling, wall to wall—wearing space around her shoulders as the walls became stitched to her skin. Light drained toward her, dimming as it neared—bent into the folds. At her chin, the drool gathered, stretched thin into a quivering membrane.

The air grew heavy, laden with the scent of iron and rain-soaked gravel. Sweat salted my lips. Cold pressed to my skin. Each drop hit the floor—sharp, steady.

My hands trembled, fingertips brushing the torn fabric of my jacket.

The sack of Yamagzhal's face stirred—wet folds flexing, twitching at the seams. The spiral inflated; pressure surged under the skin. Dozens of grainy black fingers bulged against the membrane—then hundreds—clawing outward in tides. They tore through in bursts, writhing over one another, elbows folding backward, fingers snapping in loops as they flooded the hall. They hit the floor and spread—smearing up the walls, shattering lights, cracking tile, coating everything.

I stumbled back, steel-toed tennis shoes skidding on the hardwood. The fingers multiplied—thickening, weaving into a thicket that sealed the hallway. They hit with the patter of rain hammering a tin roof. I threw up an arm in front of my face. They snaked across my wrists, over my shoulders, burrowing beneath the fabric and into the skin.

My body seized as the first of them punctured my cheek—fast, needle-sharp, punching through the bone. Another split the soft ridge beneath my eye; something else forced its way past my teeth. Black fingers shot through my elbows and into my gut, lifting me from the floor, joints locking into me like hooks. The jacket tore with my skin—fibers splitting wet, limbs pulled apart in stalks. Blood sprayed in sheets, coating my chest, slicking my thighs, puddling under my boots. The cold came with them—dry ice flooding my veins, rotting me from the core. I thrashed, boots hammering nothing, vision open and raw as fingers slid behind my eyes. My body hung limp, threaded through with black.

I swung—weak, shallow arcs pinned by the hooks through my shoulders. One finger punched through my sleeve; another slid into my side. The cold followed—coiling, winding through me, the infection tightening as it spread. My boot skidded on a slick cord of flesh beneath me; a thin strand looped my throat—tight, slicing in, blood welling.

The black crashed over me—curling high, then splashing across my body. The lights above drowned in it, dimming as I sank. Heat drained from my limbs, leaching into the floorboards.

My shoulder struck the floor, then my head thunked against the hardwood. Thorns burst behind my eyelids. Blood soaked into the wood beneath me, dark and spreading. Above, wind chimes rang— bright, brittle notes trembling through the dark.

Something tickled in my chest—light at first, then crawling, then a fluttering pressure that danced beneath my ribs. A seam curled open. One white moth slipped free—its wings broad and flat, dry quartz. It floated upward, slow against the black, the glittering body shrinking until it disappeared.

They rose in sheets from the open wound, a perfect lattice pulling itself skyward—dozens, then hundreds, their wings catching the dark as scattered frost. They blurred into a white curtain, trailing behind one another, their bodies folding into smoke. Their wings twinkled, pale flecks threading into the night. They became the stars.

Pressure built inside my head—thick, crushing, lake-black.

Eleanor sank beside me, peaceful. Her limbs dangled through the dark. Her eyes flicked toward mine.

A crack split across her forehead, webbing down her cheek. Her face went slack. A high squelch broke through the water. Blood leaked through the fracture—black, streaked with glinting blue stars.

Then she collapsed. Her face splintered, shards floating from her skull in clean, dry arcs. Her body shattered into fragments—hollow, ceramic husks. Blood bubbled up, trailing streaks of blue as it drifted. A corner of blue cloth floated nearby, the golden five-suns pin still clinging to it.

My body hung—still, pressed under the weight. We sank deeper.

There was a hole in my chest—a slit, opened clean down through the sternum. I leaned forward. My legs were gone. Inside, everything glistened; muscle peeled back, ribs cracked open. A strip of fabric floated up beside me. The lake was colder. A hand rose—mine—bruised and trembling, fingers twitching as it hovered near the wound.

Orange blood bloomed across the tattered jacket, painting the fabric in birch trees, bright orange on black. I turned it over. The birch pattern ended at the white rose stitched to the side. That stayed clean.

My fingers twitched, curling toward the torn hem of the jacket. They found the rose. The stem arced in a clean loop—tight stitch, thread dry against the pads of my fingers. I held it. The fabric crinkled.

I stroked the flower. The petals gave slightly beneath the touch—faint ridges along the edge, soft as dust. The stitching brightened with every pass—white blooming brighter, burning faint as glass in setting sunlight.

My grip weakened. The cloth split. The patch floated upward—pale, silent, turning once as it rose.

The black clung—thick, cold honey. It filled my nose, sealed my throat. The sun blinked above—dimmer, more distant.

She blotted out the light.

CHAPTER 6:

My eyelids dragged open on reluctant, rusted hinges. Darkness met me—shadows smudging the edges of my vision. The room loomed above, formless and blurry, an abyss suspended in time. Silence clung to the space, to the air drained of life. My heart pounded a drumbeat against my throbbing temples as aches gathered at the base of my neck. I blinked hard, but I couldn't pierce the haze.

My body felt wrong—angles awkward, limbs disjointed. My head throbbed in tempo with my pulse, dull and pounding. I tried to lift my hand, bound by the fatigue tethered to my skin. My gaze drifted sideways. The dark fizzed around me, bright at the edges.

The world tilted off-kilter as I forced my head to turn. Forms emerged from the dark; they peeked beyond the curtain.

I leaned forward, my eyes narrowing. The air was unbreathing, stretched flat across the floor. Silence pressed down—thick in the chest, full in the air. Sweat slid from my brow as a chill crawled up my spine. My eyes jumped, scraping across the dark, breath stalling, caught in the pressure.

I swallowed. My tongue turned dry. The room staled around me—edges smeared, sinking into the fog. I was a ripple in the stagnant air, thin and crumbling.

I shifted; muscle pulled tight—sore. My gaze latched onto the couch beneath me—uneven, listing to one side, adrift in the black sea of the room. My senses sharpened.

Cold gnawed at my skin. Sweat slicked my back. Rough fabric scratched against my cheek. I pushed myself upright; splinters teased my arm. Torn upholstery and wood beneath the frayed lining pressed firm against skin.

I strained my eyes off the side of the couch. Beneath was a black rug smeared into the floor—matte, textureless, and cold. Edges frayed and disappeared into the gloom. The floor dissolved at the edges—black bleeding into black.

He loved you.

My hand slapped against the arm of the couch, grappling for purchase. The fabric groaned beneath my cold, damp palms. I heaved upward—the coarse fibers of the couch clawed at my skin, joints creaking with the battered springs. My body rose in jerks and starts.

A shudder passed through me, cooling the sweat on my skin as I sat. My breath misted before me in the still air. The surroundings were silent but for my labored breaths. I hovered there, swaying. The hair hung in sheets across my skin. Cold seeped through my clothes, kissing my skin with icy lips.

You used him.

I steadied myself against the couch's frayed armrest. My feet planted on the floor beside the couch, curling against the carpeting of an abused rug. I moved stiffly, limbs drawn tight. My steps thudded soft against the wood. Dust motes danced away from my path, glimmers snuffed out with each stride.

The hallway loomed, a narrow gullet waiting. Floorboards stretched away into nothingness, a void hungry for warmth, for life. My gaze swept the expanse.

You're hurting him.

I shuffled forward, the chill of the planks biting into my soles through thin fabric. A shiver ran up my spine—cold, exposed.

Gloom clung to me like cobwebs. Cold air bit at my clammy skin. My clothes stuck to my body, hair plastered to my forehead.

I marched—heel to toe. My stare kept low, fixed on the floorboards.

A chill gust brushed past, ruffling the curls stuck to my neck. I flinched, goosebumps pebbling up my arms. The footfall spilled through the floor—gasping, greedy.

My hand lifted, fingertips grazing the cold sweat beading on my brow. I wiped it away. My gaze fixed on the roughness underfoot.

I staggered forward—steps fumbling into one another. My movements stuttered as the cold sank deeper. Sweat pooled beneath my ribs.

He let you in.

The wallpaper crumbled beneath my touch. My fingers trailed the tears in the paper—faded flowers, now ghosts on the wall. I rounded the corner.

My hand fell away from the wall as I passed the bathroom door, eyes pinned to my feet.

My breath clouded the chill air. The hallway ended at a final wooden door. I froze in place. My hand twitched, then sagged—weightless, useless.

I stared at the grain, dark and deep. Knots stared back. The door loomed into me, pressing forward—steel weight against my chest, squeezing breath from my lungs. The quiet throbbed—coiled tight behind my nose. My hand shot out. The metal was cold to the touch. A jiggle, a tug—nothing.

I pulled harder, veins standing out on my forearm, knuckles white; no give. A crawl set in at the base of my neck—itching, biting, frantic. It scratched and squirmed, desperate to break free. I leaned in, shoulder against wood. My breath came fast, clouds of effort puffing into the air. The door stood firm, indifferent.

You killed him.

I stepped back. My eyes darted to the cracked plaster, the lifeless hallway. I pivoted and retreated. The hallway contracted with each step. Dust particles settled, disturbed by my passage. Smoke fogged the mirror—my face blurred beneath it, body smeared. I passed the door. The corner beyond the hall snapped out of view. A room opened ahead, stillness thick. I stepped in; floorboards groaned underfoot. Wires dangled above—an empty fixture swung in slow, gentle silence.

This house isn't yours.

My gaze swept left. A couch slumped, cushions torn and leaking. A ragged blanket lay twisted beneath a scatter of empty bottles. Statuettes cast blue shadows, hummingbirds frozen mid-flight. The blue fabric of the couch was frayed and torn, cushions gutted, spilling yellow foam onto the black rug below. An orange blanket dangled, threads hanging loose like weary fingers. A low table sat in front— wood warped, edges splintered, finish worn to pulp. Tall, empty liquor bottles crowded the surface.

Across the room, a TV stand leaned against the wall, smeared with old fingerprints—oily, layered, sunken into the grain. On it, a boxy television gazed blankly into the space, surrounded by hummingbird statuettes, blue stains marring their ceramic bodies. Frames hung crooked, scattered across the walls. Inside: faces blurred and fading, features twisted, ink running through paper. My gaze skimmed the glass. A bookshelf leaned nearby—books stuffed sideways, pages torn. Their spines were cracked, titles bleached by the sun.

To my right, the kitchen loomed. A table lay laden with rot, swarms of insects scuttling and rustling through the trash. Black maggots writhed in the filth. Pills scattered across a brown, crooked table—propped beneath heaps of garbage, broken needles, and open bottles. The counters sagged under the weight. Food, blackened and shriveled, hosted a congregation of mites. They tore through the mess—fed in blind silence. Rot and spirits clung to the air—thick, sour, hooked in the back of my throat.

You haven't changed.

In the center, amidst the squalor, a single rose oozed darkness. The decay stopped short of it. The counter was sterile. Black vapor rose from its petals—thin, cold, fogging the air as it spread. Thorny folds melted, squirting and gushing. Beads of liquid clung to the bloom—thick, black, glossy with a dull gleam.

My ears caught a faint ring—thin, circling. The sound revolved around me, tightening. I clenched my jaw—bitter, brittle.

My eyes scanned the murk, my heart ticking in my chest. The room stretched—walls drifting back. The front door cracked open. I stood at the threshold, an ocean of black shifting at my feet. The floor tilted. I caught the doorframe, weight swaying with the house. My foot slipped on a board; I staggered once, then stilled.

You should leave.

The cat lay in the middle of the walkway. My peripheral vision burned out—the kitchen and living room vanished behind static. The cat stayed crisp in the dark, white and smooth, the insides of its ears black. It slept—snoring low, still. I stepped over her. She breathed in and out; the dreams had become murky.

Water dripped from the rose's stem. Cold seeped through my jacket, lingering inside of me. My feet shuffled toward the door.

I forced the black jacket over my shoulders and slid my arms inside. Crouched at the knee, I bent—scattering into my shoes beside the door. The floorboards groaned beneath me; sweat trickled. I braced a hand against the wall. Wallpaper flakes drifted—withered petals sinking to the floor. White paint hazed into black. My fingertips found the chipped wood of the doorframe.

The door loomed—warped frame, edges sunk in black. I stepped closer, drawn to the crack of night. My hand hovered—trembling—then gripped the knob. Sweat beaded across my brow. I twisted. Hinges squeaked, thin and strained. I winced. The gap widened.

But I can still love you.

I pulled the jacket tight across my chest. The door parted a hair wider; I slipped through the crack into pitch black, swallowing the shape of me. Cold pooled in my limbs. Skin tingled, then numbed. My breath caught in my throat as the pitch-blackness swallowed me whole. Cold air enveloped me, creeping beneath the jacket, raising goosebumps on my flesh. Night had devoured all light. I stepped forward, the world behind fading, the abyss before me absolute.

CHAPTER 7:

The door creaked, hanging crooked as black liquid oozed through the crack, pooling around my boots. I shoved it open; the hinges groaned under the strain. The air inside hit me—heavy, acrid, thick enough to taste. It clung to my skin, the stench sharp, burning the back of my throat. Shelves slumped into the thick black sludge that covered the floor, broken and decayed. Wires dangled from the ceiling, barely moving in the still air. Mold crept along the walls, spreading in dark patches. The coolers lining the walls stood open, glass shattered, their insides gutted. Beneath the broken tiles, the sludge clumped and shifted, swelling and receding. The counter sat in darkness, lost in the surrounding void.

"Oh," I muttered. A spike of pressure built behind my right eye. I pressed a palm to the side of my head, thumb grinding into my temple. "Fuck… Can I just— Do I get a second chance?"

Do you still think you deserve one?

Behind me, a shuffle—quick and dry, skin dragging over concrete. I turned, but the glass showed only the blackness pressed against it, as though the dark had collapsed over the station. The darkness clung to the window, thick and solid.

My boots tore through the slick black mire, each step dragging through the muck. The floor cracked with every stomp; tiles scraped against the ooze, floating up in broken chunks. I lunged for the shelf, gripping it tight—my fingers came away coated in grime. The stench burned, sharp and chemical, seeping into my skin.

The moths swarmed the back hallway, completely blocking it off—a mass revolving around the center. Fat, white, grinning with human teeth. Their wings fluttered wildly, jaws gnashing, forming a frantic wall.

Legs dangled loosely beneath the storm, arms limp at his sides. The rest of Flynt was gone, expression swallowed by a shifting swarm of moths.

I tripped on a jagged shelf edge. Pain tore through my ankle as I hit the floor, metal biting into skin. Blood ran hot, then froze, creeping in with the numbness. Black sludge splattered, sinking into my jacket—heavy. I shoved myself up, gasping, and staggered toward Flynt.

"Flynt!" My voice barely cut through the thick air. He hung still, limp, moths clinging to his face. I seized his arm and yanked.

He sagged into me, dead weight. The moths clung to him, crawling and shifting, their bodies plastered to his skin. When I pulled him, they followed.

I yanked harder—hands trembling, arms locked—dragging him out of the hallway. His body slumped into mine, shoulders sagging under my grip. I stared at his eyes—wide, vacant, unfocused. His gaze was hollow. Buried within the reflection of his eyes was an empty room: concrete walls, cold and bare. A single bulb swung overhead, throwing thin light. Shadows crept across the floor, twisting, shifting with life. Flynt's lips twitched, creeping open. A dead rasp slipped from his lips, distant.

My gaze clung to his—trapped in that concrete room, frozen under a dim, rocking bulb. My breath slowed. The world beyond froze; dust hung in place. My heart stalled. One heartbeat, ten heartbeats, a hundred—I sank deeper into his reflection.

Then I shook. My legs shook. Fingernails dug into his arm. I forced my vision out of that room, back to myself. Releasing his shoulder, I shoved. He pressed into the wall, shoulder-first; I stumbled back, teeth clenched, breath ragged.

The darkness swallowed the end of the hallway, devouring it inch by inch, until there was nothing but a void where the exit had been. The edges bled into blackness. Moths circled tighter, their wings brushing Flynt's face, gathering on him. The air hung thick with damp rot.

Beyond the hallway, the world dissolved. Everything outside this narrow strip turned black. A faint orange glow flickered from the elevator at the side, casting its dim light across the stretch of tile for a fleeting moment before fading.

The moths settled on Flynt, still perched on his lips, his eyes—unmoving. My chest tightened. Cold crept down the hall, familiar and biting. The hallway grew longer—pulling, twisting, stretching until the end seemed impossibly distant.

I turned, my neck stiff, the movement slow and unnatural, a creak in the joints. My gaze locked on the darkness behind me. The black tiles dried without a sound. Wood crept across the floor—dark, seeping, swallowing tile as it went. The walls twisted, wallpaper unfurling like skin peeling back, consuming the concrete, until the station itself seemed to vanish.

Rotting wood strangled the walls, swallowing the gas station's peeling paneling. It clawed toward the bathroom door. Metal groaned; rust flaked off in heavy sheets, exposing brittle veins of wood beneath. A flaky creak followed—the bathroom sign crashed to the floor. Twisting with a wheeze, the frame warped, left jagged and split.

My breath hitched. I reached for Flynt's wrist, grabbing it hard, fingers grinding into his limp shirt, smearing tar-black sludge across the fabric. Moths swarmed over his skin—black-bellied and swollen, crawling across his face. Their legs scraped his cheeks, packed tight against his skin, writhing in slow waves.

The air thickened. A deep creak split the room as the bathroom door shifted. I couldn't blink. It groaned, hinges dragging in stutters.

Rot clung to the doorframe as I nudged it open with the knuckle of my free hand. The door creaked, uneven on its hinges, the sound sharp in the suffocating quiet. Flynt's wrist was slick in my grip, his body limp, following mindlessly. Moths covered his face, their legs writhing and gnashing across his skin, toothy grins packed together in a thick, pulsing mass. He staggered, head tilted, like he was dangling from strings.

Inside, the bathroom was thick with a choking blackness, the air wet and sickly, stinking of mildew. My boots squelched over the floor as my eyes strained against the dark, drawing shapes from the murk. A grimy sink sagged against the far wall, a crooked mirror hanging above it. In the reflection—my face: hollow cheeks, curls limp and tangled, skin drawn tight with exhaustion. Black sludge streaked my jacket, thick and sticky, devouring the embroidered white rose. But the mirror was spotless.

Cracked tiles sprawled underfoot, jagged edges cutting into my soles. Shallow troughs lined the walls, overflowing with congealed filth, crumpled wrappers, and dead insects. Thin roots snaked through the muck, twitching. The light above dangled useless, its exposed wires twitching like nerves.

A dull thump rang out—sudden and graceless. Braelyn crouched in the corner, knees sunk in a shallow black puddle, her thin blonde hair standing in wild, uneven tufts, streaked with splotches of black. The green uniform was stained with filth, skin smeared and blotchy. Bloodshot eyes stared wide and unfocused, lips quivering, baring crooked teeth—some missing, the rest blackened like rotting wood. She clawed at her scalp, nails digging deep. Pitch-black blood oozed in thick rivulets down her temples. Her head jerked back, and more of it slid behind her neck, vanishing into the collar of that filthy uniform. White moths fluttered from the hallway, fast and erratic. They swarmed Flynt's face, landing on his eyes, his lips. I grabbed him by the wrist, dragging his limp body deeper into the bathroom. The tiles beneath Braelyn sagged, warping as the black sludge clung to her legs, streaking her skin. I reached toward her.

"Braelyn." The word fell dead.

Braelyn slammed into the wall again, head cracking against the tile. The surrounding fluid rippled, swirling with rotting trash, wrapping around her ankles. Bloodshot eyes widened, then fogged. Drool collected at her lips, stringing down her chin as she kicked at the floor; black ooze splashed up against the cracked tiles.

"Braelyn," I muttered again, pulling away—useless.

I dragged Flynt deeper into the room. He staggered, the moths clinging tighter to his skin, their toothy grins twitching. The writhing swarm buried his eyes. The sound drove into my skull, relentless, sharp.

I glanced back at the mirror. Flynt stood beside me, the moths still writhing over his face, their bodies pulsing. My reflection wasn't mine anymore. Staring back at me from the glass was Yamagzhal's mask—a flat white ceramic rabbit, with long, straight ears pointing rigidly upward, rounded at the tips. A crudely drawn black face grinned back— no eyes, no mouth, no holes. The mask pressed flush against my skin.

I blinked, my breath catching in my throat. My hand shot up to my face, trembling, but my fingers met only flesh. I felt my cheek, my jaw—warm skin beneath my fingertips. But in the mirror, there I was, wearing Yamagzhal's mask, expressionless. I looked down at Braelyn, still broken.

I stormed forward, boots skidding on the tile. My reflection held still, the rabbit mask grinning at the center of the glass. I bumped into the sink—cold porcelain against my stomach—as I leaned in. Behind the figure, another bathroom waited: white light pouring over a narrow shower on the left and a fogged sink and mirror to the right. I leaned closer. The figure didn't move. Somewhere behind the glass, water dripped—slow and constant.

My hand rose—slow, shaking. I pressed through the glass. Fingers curled tight around the collar of her jacket, knuckles whitening. She lifted her hand—smooth—and laid it against my cheek. It was me in the mirror, but the touch of my own skin was pins and needles.

Her nails pressed into my cheek—slow at first, then deep. I gripped her collar harder. A sharp sting bloomed as one nail pierced the surface. I froze as the pain flared beneath my skin, blood trickling down my cheek.

Braelyn's breath stopped short, chest hitching, silent. Her eyes locked on mine—wide, hollow.

My reflection hesitated for a moment, then dragged her nail down, tearing open the flesh. Heat seared through my jaw, deep and hot. Orange-tinted blood clung to her fingernail, then streamed down my upper arm in slow, steady grooves. It gathered at the crook of my elbow before dripping to the tile. Braelyn's eyes stayed locked, wide, watching the skin curl back. The blood soaked through my sleeve, warm and thick.

The reflection carved a slow circle along my jaw—then my cheekbone, then my forehead—shearing flesh, embedding into muscle. I shot a hand up, shoving at her shoulder, feet kicking back against the sink basin. Her grip tightened, fingers locked in place. The rest of her held still; only the hand moved.

The skin fell away in a slow, wet revolution, hanging there for a second before dropping to the floor with a sickening thud.

Braelyn sat trembling in the corner, rubbing her eyes with her filthy sleeve, her green uniform streaked with snot and tears. "El-Eleanor—she's—she's dead." She was small, rocking, her eyes wide and fixed on the orange stain pooling around my feet.

The mask stared straight ahead—still, unblinking. The drawn-on smile stretched taller; the eyes pinched at the edges. It giggled—shoulders bouncing, one hand rising to its chin. Then it shoved me backward. I tripped over the sheet of flesh beneath my feet and slammed onto the tile. When I looked up, the mirror reflected the bathroom: Flynt's head swarming with moths, a few perched on either sink edge—grinning toothily in the dim light—alongside Braelyn. My reflection was gone.

I stumbled toward Braelyn, every nerve in my face screaming with raw, burning pain. The heat clawed down my neck, spreading into my chest. My vision blurred, the room swaying as I extended my hand toward her, blood coating my fingers.

"Godfrey's…uh—" I swallowed, throat locking. "He's downstairs, right?" The words dragged, caught in my throat.

Braelyn cocked her head, wiping tears off her cheek with her sleeve. "Y-you remember?"

Braelyn's shaky hand reached out, grasping mine. Her fingers were icy, trembling as they curled around my blood-soaked skin. Her other hand wrapped around my sleeve, pulling herself up, her legs quaking beneath her. The earring hung off her hand—the black, blood-streaked chain looped tight around the meat of her thumb. She leaned into me, her body trembling, breath shallow and ragged. My jacket strained under the pressure, but I didn't move. Wings battered my hand. The air buzzed, thick with moths.

"So…uh…how do we get there?" I asked, rubbing the back of my neck.

Braelyn jerked, a dead, twitching flinch. Her head tilted, slow— then she nodded, her chin almost brushing my shoulder. "A-ah! W-we have to take the elevator down to his room!"

They were both close. Braelyn's body pressed warm against my side, fingers slicking my jacket with black sludge. Flynt was right there too—his face gone, swallowed by the moths. The fluttering mass tickled my cheek, their wings soft, a brush of fine paper. The heat of them wafted through my jacket.

I shoved the bathroom door open. Moisture slicked the wooden frame, smeared under my palm—foreign against the tile.

Moths slammed into us, their wings flickering in the dim light, moving in bursts. White wings beat at my face, their tiny bodies bursting with the black liquid that smeared across my skin. I squinted, boots sinking into wet grime. Braelyn dragged behind me, her grip locked on my sleeve.

We stepped into the hallway. Faded floral wallpaper streaked the walls, peeling back to expose the gas station's gray rot. Warped floorboards creaked, wet with oil and something thicker. Across the hall, the steel mesh elevator door waited. Lights flickered above, casting a sick brown glow—too weak to push through the dark. Braelyn's breath hit the back of my neck, fast and shallow. She stumbled, half-walking, clinging to my arm.

I glanced back. Flynt followed, his face swallowed by the moths. Wings crawled over his skin, shifting and pulsing. He shrugged them off without a word, trudging through the sludge like it didn't touch him.

"Flynt," I called, my voice scraping through the hum of wings. He didn't answer, his shadow trailing behind. The elevator loomed a step away.

At the far end of the hallway, beyond the failing lights, something stood. She towered beyond the station's hall—shoulders high above the rafters. Her bloated spine scraped the flaking plaster, body pinched flat yet swelled with severed knots.

Mid-hall, a rabbit mask hung in the dark—white ceramic, scribbled over in black marker, mouth trembling with the faint twitch of breath. It tracked me, head tilting, staring. The walls bent to her focus.

Flynt stood still. Moths coated his head in shifting layers—bodies crawling over his scalp, legs catching at his lashes, wings brushing his jaw. They pulsed around him, a wet, breathing shell. He turned with a stiff drag of his neck. The movement stirred them. Down the corridor, Yamagzhal flickered in the dark. A single moth broke loose, then two, then a ribbon—fluttering off-balance, wings stuttering. The mass followed. A soft patter filled the air, dry and frantic. They tumbled toward her in a wavering stream, smacking into her hair; they slipped between strands and sank, silent, vanishing inside.

My fingers stabbed at the elevator button, jabbing it over and over. The sound was a rapid, hollow *click-click-click* that echoed in the vast emptiness of the gas station. The steel mesh door stood firm. Silence engulfed us—seemed to crawl under the skin. I locked into the elevator. A cavernous black maw stared back. The far side held the faint shape of a mesh barrier, a ghostly outline in the murky darkness. My gaze never left the doors. Heel tapped next—grinding into the soaked floor, fluid seeping into the grooves of my shoes; fingers hovered near the button, twitchy.

The station quivered. A muffled rumble crept up my spine, the flickering lights casting my shadow in jerking motions. Fluorescents above spasmed, hammering down in snaps of cold light.

Each burst of light revealed more—the toppled shelves, the bags bobbing in black ooze, the white moths gnashing their teeth in ravenous hunger.

"Shit," I muttered. The building trembled again—a deep surge rising through the tile.

The elevator loomed ahead—silent and still. The button's glow faded as another shudder passed through the gas station. Dust and small debris sprinkled from the ceiling, dancing in the air before settling on the surface of the black fluid. My hand tensed. My nostrils flared.

The mesh lurched, metal shrieking as it pulled apart. Grates stuttered open, one after the other, each hinge jerking in slow recoil. Rust flaked loose, scraped down the frame. Something foul slid out with the dark—oily, close. I stepped in. Breath pulled thin over my tongue, tinged with metal.

Moths swept into the elevator—white wings fluttering in erratic spirals, teeth gnashing. They clung to the grate, drawn by the light that flickered overhead. I stepped in first, my boots squelching in puddles. The black fluid clung to me, tar seeping into the treads. Flynt followed, his sandals making wet slaps against the metal floor. His eyes scanned the corners. The moths landed on him, their bodies pulsating, but he brushed them off with a detached swipe. Braelyn shuffled in—hunched, small, her shoulders curled tight. Her shoes sank into the liquid; it lapped over her soles as she dragged forward. Each step thickened, slower than the last. She slumped against the wall by the buttons, breath hitching through clenched teeth.

The button clicked under Braelyn's trembling finger. Purple numbers lit up, one after another. Her gaze never lifted from the floor, fixated on the dark reflection staring back at her.

The elevator ground into motion—a slow, dragging descent. Metal doors clacked shut, sealing us in. Braelyn didn't move. Her head hung low, shoulders trembling. Breath rasped through her nose, shallow and fast. Black fluid seeped between the panels, dripping into thin streams. It struck the floor in wet, irregular slaps—echo swallowed by the steel.

My shoulder scraped against Braelyn's as the elevator shuddered, steel grinding beneath our feet. The air thickened—choked with the sour, greasy reek of black film smeared across the walls. My breath caught; lungs filled like sludge, steeped in sour corrosion, raw and constant. Flynt bumped against my other side. My hand reached out, fingers brushing cold metal and damp skin. I turned my head—darkness smudged the edges. A moth veered close, wings twitching wild across my cheek. I batted it away; its bristled body scraped my palm before it dropped.

The walls seemed to close in, the space narrowing even as we continued to plummet. My gaze caught on the panels above, where the only light flickered—a dying star dripping light into a crust of black.

Another jolt hit—metal screamed as the elevator scraped the walls. Flynt's sandal slipped against the slick floor. I caught the wall, palm smearing across wet steel. Filth clung—oily, grainy, thick enough to coat the nailbeds. My jaw set.

The chill soaked the seams of my clothing, pooled on my knees, and needled into my spine. I leaned away from the corner of the elevator.

Something beyond, there in the murk, unfolded itself from the floor—slumped, head down. Something pale and skinny stood there, flesh pocked with holes crusted in dried black filth. My breath hitched. Steel-toed shoes edged backward as it stirred. It rose without sound, weightless. Its back scraped against the wall, a faint grating noise barely perceptible over the elevator's lament. The air grew colder. My fingers curled into fists, nails biting palms. Sweat pearled on my brow despite the chill. Eyes fixed on the figure, I stepped closer to Flynt. Its ascent was slow. Each movement was an aberration. My throat tightened, but no sound escaped.

Braelyn's head snapped to the rustling, a deep dragging sound. Her back went rigid, pressing cold against the metal wall. Wide eyes cut through the dark, fixed on the corner where deathly silence had been. It rose—slow, joints cracking—as the body stretched higher, spine dragging upward past the top of the frame, limbs folding to fit.

I staggered back, soles slipping against the muck. Its head pressed against the ceiling; ribs flexed, scraped the wall, skin catching on the seams of the paneling.

A specter that stumbled forward, limbs askew, joints knocking in arrhythmic jerks, it scraped along the floor in a slow, awkward scramble. Black fluid surged ahead, rippling toward us. My hand found the wall, fingers scraping over steel as I edged away. Its steps dragged forward—slow, deliberate, sloshing through the black. Flynt stood motionless beside me, his outline vague in the murk. The air pressed close, dense and stinking, thick in the throat. The creature's form blurred at the edges—half-swallowed by dark, shifting with the sway of the light.

Nearer now, the darkness seemed to peel away from its face. Features emerged, starting in broad strokes—Eleanor's face, pale and gaunt, hovered in the gloom.

"Sorry," it whispered. The voice, high and creaking, fractured the silence. "I'm sorry, I'm sorry."

I recoiled, breath hitching. The words echoed off the walls. Eleanor's dead eyes bore into Braelyn's, unblinking, unseeing.

"Let's go home." Louder now—rising through the static. Its mouth twitched, slack and loose in the sockets, jaw hitching—teeth clacking. I stepped back, foot slipping in the sludge.

"I'm still here." Over and over. The whisper seemed to come from everywhere, closing in. My pulse hammered in my ears, tangled in the rhythm of that voice.

Her stride staggered—footfalls tangled. Arms hung loose, fingers twitching. It shambled forward, limbs jerking out of time, twitching to realign with the sway. Braelyn's back hit the steel mesh of the elevator door. She pressed hard against it, as if she could meld into the metal and escape. Her eyes locked, pupils blown. Breath skimmed fast through parted lips, chest hitching with each drag.

"We can go back." Sound grated—sharp, scraping through the air. Beneath us, the elevator lurched; metal trembled. Mesh dug into Braelyn's skin, leaving angry red impressions.

"Hold my hand." Closer now—the figure's face—Eleanor's loomed over Braelyn, eyes empty, mouth a gash. Braelyn's lips parted, soundless. Her hands fumbled behind her.

"Sorry." *Thud.* The elevator shook. Dust fell like ash from above. The light flickered, a dying heartbeat. "Sorry, dear."

The figure lurched, a disjointed topple. It collided with Braelyn, a dead weight that pinned her to the steel mesh. Her breath hitched, pinned beneath the carcass.

"Hon, I miss you," it whispered, the voice of Eleanor fractured by a high pitch.

"Please," Braelyn's voice trembled out, a thread thin enough to snap.

Braelyn's gaze fixed on Eleanor's body, her eyes wide, rims catching the flicker. Her throat bulged unnaturally, the skin stretching around an emerging shape, sharp and jagged. The crack of bone and rending flesh filled the elevator as her jaw distended—hinges popping wide, skin stretching to rupture. Black blood oozed, thick and viscous, dribbling down her chin. It mingled with tears and sweat. Her lips split, flesh tearing in stringy webs.

From Braelyn's gaping maw, thin black appendages writhed out, slick with mucus and twitching against the air. They curled from the body, twisting like torn muscle. Dozens of them, slick with the same dark ichor that pooled at her feet, reached out to caress the walls. A mass emerged from her throat, dragged into the world by the squirming limbs. It pushed against the confines of her mouth, stretching the torn edges farther, spilling out beneath the dimming light.

The black chicken crowded the elevator, its bulk pressed against walls streaked with filth. Legs—long, hair-thin, bundled tight, then splaying wide—slick and countless, always moving, snaked across the floor, tapping at corners, scraping metal. Light flickered; limbs caught it in flashes, casting tangled motion across the muck. Beady eyes stared through the dark—unblinking, sunk deep in pulsing sockets.

Braelyn hit the floor hard—limbs slack, head tilted back. Her mouth hung open, skin stretched thin across the jaw. No pupils. Just milky glaze. Through the gape, the back of her throat showed the wall behind her. The body lay still—dry, collapsed in on itself.

I shoved at Flynt, my hands slipping against the soaked sheet clinging to his back. One of the chicken's legs skimmed my arm— thin, jointed, damp like a roach. I recoiled; it mopped forward, legs tripping over legs, dragging slick across the floor. The air thickened around it—dense with heat, feathers grazing skin, grease clinging in the lungs.

The Eleanor-figure crumpled, the onslaught of writhing appendages overpowering her. She hit the floor, the impact a dull thud against the metal grate. Her body lay still, arms splayed. My breath came in sharp gasps, swallowed by the wet patter of its skittering legs. But the walls closed in, reality distorting within. I lunged for the doors, my fingers finding the cold comfort of the mesh.

The elevator shuddered. My hand stilled on the mesh, my gaze snapping to the lifeless form beneath the tall black chicken—Eleanor spread beneath a canopy of writhing legs. Pale and gaunt, talons dropped—curved, yellowed, crusted with muck. They tore into soft meat, ripping, pulling at the fabric of something half-formed. Pale chunks fell away. The stomach burst open; a grotesque bloom of innards spilled out. I flinched, bile rising. The smell hit me, sharp and metallic—talons worked, extracting flesh and bone. The fat jiggled, then split under the assault.

The chicken, monstrous and dripping, bent its head low. White tongues emerged, pale against the darkness, writhing worms in the eye of a corpse. They reached for Eleanor, slithering over her body with grotesque intimacy. Sucking noises filled the elevator, wet and thick, as the tongues slurped black fluid pooling inside the torn flesh.

The world jerked. A crunch snapped up through the floor—metal buckling deep below. The elevator groaned, scraped to a halt. I staggered into the wall. Overhead, a warped chime blurted out, crackling into static. The grate ahead shuddered in its frame. Beyond it: a concrete room, black as oil, light bleeding off at the threshold. Flynt didn't move, his glassy stare fixed forward.

The doors jittered, a metallic rattle against silence. They clung to their frame, stubborn, unmoving. I surged forward. My hands slammed against the mesh, fingers scraping metal. A sharp clink echoed as I yanked at the unyielding barrier. The steel resisted, cold biting into my palms, slick with frost. Breath fogged between clenched teeth, curling up into the stillness. Outside, black pressed in—thick, depthless, unmoving. My grip tightened, knuckles blanching. I pulled again, muscles pulled taut, joints popping in protest. The door held.

Veins bulged down my arms as I seized the mesh—steel rough against my palms, flakes of rust catching at the skin. It shivered under my grip. I slammed the door back and forth; a rattling grind surged through the shaft, the clatter sharp, teeth-on-metal. The frame jolted in place. I shoved forward, shoulder locking into the bars, pressure roaring through bone and joint. A second hit—harder—sent a dull ache through my lungs. The door trembled again but didn't give. Cold bled through the metal, sunk into my hands. Rust licked the air.

My gaze dropped. The black fluid, thick and oozing, clung to my shoes. It crawled up the leather, a living stain seeking skin. Heat radiated from the soles, seeping through to my flesh. A numbness spread, insidious, deadening the pain. I kicked at the liquid, sending droplets splashing against the elevator walls. They sizzled where they landed, pockmarking the surface with fresh scars.

The black sloshed shallow across the elevator floor—glossed, stinking, pooled in swells that lapped the mesh. Ripples dragged across the surface in lazy intervals, pulled by some current deeper than the car. Each wave rolled slowly, brushing the grate with a soft slap, then drawing back in a smear of muck and grit. Trash floated inside: shredded wrappers, wet gauze, broken bits of plastic, all drifting in uneven loops.

My hand hung beside it. Trembling, I glanced down. Fluid reflected the outline—knuckles twitching, fingers curled toward the palm. Pale scars climbed along the skin like bone-white roots. I turned sharply, weight shifting into one hip.

"Flynt, the—uh—the soda. You got it?" He blinked—slow, flat. His hand slid into his pocket with a twist of his shoulder. Fabric rustled. Out came the Yamagzhal soda, gripped in his slender hand. The label glinted—flecks of gold catching stray light. My eyes locked on the bottle.

His fingers curled around the cap, twisting. A faint hiss as pressure released, carbonation seething in the dark. The bottle rose, dragging through thick air. I sprang.

"Flynt!" My voice cut through the gloom, hoarse and sharp.

I crashed into him, shoulder first, knees clipping his thigh, fingers clawing at the fabric, breath hot between us. The wall of the elevator gave way to our momentum, metal clanging under the impact.

"Give it!" I said, hand snatching for the drink. His grip tightened, wrist twisting away from my grasping fingers—bottle to lips, liquid poised at the edge. I drove my palm into his chest, slammed him back—his head struck metal, breath jolted loose.

"It's mine," he muttered, but I was already wrenching the soda free. Flynt hunched over, chest heaving. My hands shook, sweat cooling fast on my skin. The hum of the elevator pressed up through our soles—steady, rumbling, unbroken.

Soda fizzed, splattered across my hand. Skin seared, a sharp bite amidst the grapple. Flynt's eyes widened just a notch, flicking to the drops as they hissed against my skin.

"Fuck…" I muttered, jerking the bottle away. I turned, breath ragged, and charged toward the grated door. The liquid sloshed as I stumbled through the dark fluid, steel-toed shoes sliding slick through the muck.

I upended the bottle, liquid cascading over metal. The acid soda worked fast, eating into the grating with a venomous hiss. Smoke rose, acrid and biting, in the cramped air of the elevator. The metal sizzled, edges glowing faintly as they gave way to corrosion.

"My drink…" Flynt's voice was soft.

My hands clamped onto the fizzing metal, fingers weaving through the mesh. The door buckled, the acid-softened wires giving way beneath my relentless grip. I pulled—muscles taut, veins standing out against my skin.

"Are you fucking stupid?" Metal groaned above—deep, warped, grinding through the frame. Bolts shifted in their housings. Steel popped, flexed. "Fuck your drink."

I yanked again, harder this time. Mesh tore into jagged, biting edges. Sweat beaded on my forehead, dripped into my eyes, stung like the soda on my hand. I heaved at the weakened grating; the hole widened under my assault. Smoke swirled, clawed at my throat with invisible talons. My breath came in short, fierce bursts, misting in the air before me. My arms flexed, another violent tug, the door yielding inch by grudging inch. Metal screeched, cried out its last defiance—shoulder twisting deeper until the frame gave.

Flynt's gaze dropped to the crumpled form on the elevator floor. "She's fine."

I crouched down, my hands hovering over Braelyn's mangled face. Despite the slack weight of her body, her fingers still clutched the earring—its edges dug into her palm. A canine whimper came from behind the wall—clipped short, begging.

"Braelyn…" My fingers grazed the torn flesh, recoiling at the wetness. Silence pounded in my ears. Flynt shifted, his shadow falling over us. His eyes were empty pools, reflecting nothing.

"Uh—help me." I jerked my chin. "Uh…just like we used to."

The black chicken squawked—sharp, wet. Legs twitched in sequence, shifting weight across the glistening floor. Its head jerked up. Beady black eyes snapped to Flynt, unblinking. A string of gut hung slack from its beak, swaying.

Its gaze locked—neck stiff, whole body tilted toward him.

Then a claw curled. Then another. The body beneath it twitched as more viscera peeled free, raked across the tile. A loop caught on bone; the chicken yanked. Wet sounds filled the air—slick, dragging, thick with breath. Its pupils tracked him in tiny jerks—measured, avian, constant.

Flynt stepped around the heaving bird-thing, bulk slick with fluid, legs writhing out in twitching tangles. It crouched over Eleanor—what scraps remained—pale skin split open, blue uniform bunched and soaked, limbs drawn in piece by piece. Her spine bent backward with a wet crack as the chicken's beak plunged again.

Flynt reached for Braelyn's shoulders, fingers slipping beneath the damp fabric, hoisting her with a grunt. The creature kept feeding—head jerking, eyes fixed on the mess beneath it, beak dragging gore into its throat. I stumbled in, dropped to one knee. My hands wrapped tight around Braelyn's ankles—scrubs soaked, cold, bunched in my grip. I pulled. Her weight hit hard. Shoulders burned. My arms locked at the elbows.

Fabric tore behind us, louder than breath. The floor squelched, liquid slapping against my boots. I pushed up, legs trembling, and lifted. She slipped; I readjusted, jaw clenched. We staggered forward, her feet dragging deep ruts through the muck. My wrists screamed.

The elevator mesh bit into my arm. Beyond it, the dark held— thick, still, untouched by the flickering light. We inched closer. My grip tightened around Braelyn's legs.

We crouched again. Flynt grunted as his fingers slipped under Braelyn's arms; I grabbed behind her knees, fabric soaked through and clinging. Her body shifted between us—cold, slick, sagging. My shoulder pressed into her thigh as we hoisted her up. Fluid squelched underfoot. Her weight dragged crooked across our backs, spine twisting under the load.

I adjusted first, sliding a hand higher along her leg. The meat gave slightly under my grip. Flynt stepped back. My boots skidded in the black—a slap of liquid, a crack in my shoulder. Her arm dropped, smacking the floor with a wet clap. Black fluid splashed up my shin.

Moths clung thick along the walls—layered rows of them perched like fungus, wings closed in still sheets, their bodies twitching with slow rhythm. Their scales caught the flicker of overhead light, pale and powdery, framing a thousand shivering smiles stamped into the dark. When they moved, they moved together—an uneasy ripple down the shaft, soft legs scraping metal as they shifted place by place.

Black fluid dripped from above, each strand drawn long before it fell—slow, deliberate, bursting wet across the floor. The splatter bounced in layers, rippling out over the muck. Air shifted with every impact; a soft pulse traveled across the surface.

Light sputtered overhead. On the floor, my shadow stretched thin—an orange lattice warped across the sheen, faint and trembling where it floated on the muck. Flynt's shape was gone. Braelyn's had no trace.

We moved again—weight slipping down my hips, her body slick in my arms. My grip cinched hard around the fabric at her knees. Braelyn shifted; a jolt ran through my side. Her heel struck bone—sharp—left a hollow throb in my ribs. Breath tore up raw from my chest as we lurched forward. The mesh edged near—twisted steel laced with rust, corners dulled but catching flickers of orange from the light above, bent outward like split teeth.

We reached the gap. The melted steel smoked faintly; a smear of rust and black lined the edge. The dark behind it held still.

We twisted Braelyn's body toward the gap, her limbs slack against our arms. The mesh dug in—sharp teeth biting through the cloth, dragging thin cuts along her ribs. I dropped my shoulder, shoved under her side. Flynt leaned in; she shifted, rolled, caught halfway.

Steel scraped down her back. Her shirt pulled, stretched, then tore with a dry rip. I braced against her thigh, pushed again—metal groaned as she slid through. One foot snagged, then ripped free.

She fell. Her body lurched forward—limp, arms trailing, head tipping fast. Fabric whispered past the torn steel. She struck the concrete headfirst. The crack echoed.

A thin dog-whine carried through the elevator shaft.

My hands hit the edge. Cold, wet metal smeared my skin. I pulled up, boots scrabbling for purchase. A burr caught my palm—split skin. I swung one leg through, torso pressed tight to the frame, jacket dragging rough against the mesh. My jacket snagged. I jerked, off-balance; thread gave. I twisted, crouched, and shoved the rest of my weight forward. My ribs scraped against the opening as I spilled through, boots planting flat.

Flynt followed. He ducked low, moved smooth—no catch, no drag—clothes brushing quietly against the grate. His sandals hit the concrete just behind mine. Darkness swallowed everything past the floor. Light died across the walls. Black slicked the ground.

I ran a hand down my chest—fabric clung, warm spots pulsed where skin broke. My other hand found the floor—rough concrete, sharp at the seams. Breath came tight. Shoulders rose hard. The air tasted stale, thick with metal and sweat.

Flynt stood just ahead, his outline soft. I tracked along my arms—burnt patches, torn sleeves. The concrete buzzed beneath us. A quiet hum climbed through our soles, into the spine. My chest tightened. The hum grew louder.

CHAPTER 8:

The stench hit—thick, rancid air clogged with mold and rot, piss festering in the walls. My boot sank into something soft. A wet squelch echoed, smothered by the heavy, unmoving air. I kicked it; something swollen shifted beneath the sheet. Flynt stood still beside me, his vague silhouette bleeding into the concrete.

My eyes adjusted, picking out details in the gloom. Sheets and rags littered the floor, soaked, tangled, sticky. Rotting furniture slumped in piles, swollen with decay. Dust floated through the air, catching faint light, but the walls remained distant, unreachable. Despite the clutter, the room was a void—something in it pulling away, empty. It had swallowed itself.

I stepped forward. The floor clung to my soles. Braelyn lay in the center, limbs twisted, half-buried under damp rags. Her uniform stuck to her, soaked through, limp and lifeless. I crouched, touched her freezing shoulder.

"Fuck." I straightened up, breath catching. The weight of the room pressed in, choking, thick. Flynt was nothing more than a shadow beside me, swallowed by the emptiness. The echoes of our breaths had painted the room pitch-black. My fingers curled into fists at my sides, nails digging into my palms.

The bulb fizzed to life above us, washing over the room in uneven strokes. It threw shadows that jerked across the concrete walls, leaving some corners dim, others glaring under the weak glow. Dust drifted through the air, clinging to the stale light.

Clothes lay scattered across the floor. Hoodies, skirts, uniforms— every type of fabric twisted together in piles, soaked in black sludge, crusted with filth. Socks glued to the concrete. Decay drowned the colors—slimy, ruined—choking the entire room.

Against the far wall, broken furniture was crammed tight—chairs sagging with rot, legs splintered, a dresser bloated and split open. Mold crawled over the wood, swollen, about to burst. But the room was still empty.

The bed swallowed the back of the room, massive and unnatural, layered with thick blankets. They tangled together in a mess of colors, all torn and soaked through, twisted into one thick, suffocating mass. The stench rising from it clung to my throat. Underneath, something bulged—hidden.

Braelyn lay twisted on the floor, almost forgotten in the wreckage. Her face hung torn, jaw hanging by thin strips of flesh, her cheeks ripped down to the bone. Black blood seeped from her, thick and slow, pooling beneath her head. Her uniform was soaked in it, glued to her skin. Her eyes were wide, fixed on the elevator doors.

I blinked, the cold air scratching at my throat. My stomach clenched, but I didn't flinch. The light flickered again, casting Braelyn's ruined face in and out of shadow. My boots pulled at the floor, the filth sticking with every step. The room closed in, still hollow.

Flynt stood still, his eyes locked on Braelyn. The light flickered once more, shadows jumping before it settled.

The bed heaved. A shape beneath the blankets swelled, pushing the fabric up like something rotting struggling to the surface. The sheets twisted, the whole mass rising. A swollen form erupted from it, gasping for air.

His body was bloated, slick with sweat, his skin pale and freckled. He was hairless except for the square mustache plastered to his upper lip, twitching as he panted. His eyes darted around, wild, before locking onto me. He lay sprawled across the bed, every inch of him exposed, his flabby chest gleaming in the dull light, folds of skin settling heavily against his legs and stomach.

"Who are you people?" he rasped, his voice cutting through the silence, whiny and shrill.

He sat there, feet tangled in the mess of blankets, staring at me, then licked his cracked lips. His gaze roamed over me, lingering.

"Great. Another one." He laughed, but it came out wet, like he was choking on it. His tongue flicked across his teeth.

My fists clenched at my sides, but I didn't move. The air was thick, stagnant, pressing down. He kept staring, waiting for something, his eyes glazed and watery, a dying fish.

"Godfrey?" It scraped up my throat, my stomach tightening as I spoke. The word left a cold, oily taste in my mouth.

He grunted, flopping back into the mound of blankets, digging through the mess. Something metallic caught the light—he pulled out a revolver, wiping his greasy fingers over the barrel. The sight of it twisted my stomach, pulling tight like a fist. I knew that gun.

"It worked for him…" Godfrey whined, voice trembling as he held the gun in both hands, like it was something sacred. "Why won't it work for me?" His lip quivered as he stared at it, then, without warning, he shoved the barrel into his mouth. His hand shook as he wrapped his finger around the trigger. Before I could react, he pulled it.

The shot cracked through the room, echoing off the concrete walls. The lights flickered off, leaving us in darkness for a breath. Then they sputtered back on.

Blood had sprayed across the walls, streaks of orange-red smeared along the bed, flecks tangled in the blankets and scattered across the filthy clothes covering the floor. Flaps of skin stuck to the bedframe, caught in the crusted sheets. His skull had caved in for a moment, then mended itself—his bloated face was whole again, untouched, still breathing. He sat there, his breath ragged, gun in hand.

"Didn't work," he croaked, a brittle whisper. His voice cracked, thin and pathetic. His shoulders sagged, then shook, a weak sob crawling up his throat. One hand smeared across his bloated cheeks—sweat and tears blending into a disgusting mess. "Why won't it work?" His words came out broken. "It's not fair."

He threw the gun down onto the bed, a shrill, high-pitched scream tearing from his throat. He slammed his fists into the blankets, shaking them loose, throwing them around in a tantrum.

He looked up at me with bloodshot, swollen eyes, his lip trembling as he sniffled, wiping his nose on the back of his hand.

"It's not fucking fair. Everything's shit. No one cares about any-thing." His voice wavered, climbing to a whine. "No one's supposed to be stuck here. I'm not supposed to be stuck here."

I stood there, silent. My nails dug into my palms, fists clenched tight. The gun gleamed on the bed beside him, its sightline etched painfully into my mind. My throat clenched, bile rising thick and bitter, but I swallowed it down.

Godfrey sobbed into his hands, his massive form shaking with every wet breath, his body a pathetic lump in the middle of the room. His words broke into nothing, swallowed by the slick, ragged sounds of his crying. The light flickered again, throwing jagged shadows over him, every flash making his bloated body more twisted, more unreal.

His flesh quivered, snot and sweat dripping off his face, his cheeks wet and red from his hands wiping at them. He sat there, soaked in filth, and for a second the entire room seemed to hold its breath, waiting for him to collapse into himself.

I didn't move—didn't say a word. My eyes locked onto him, this disgusting, fat lump of flesh in front of me. His body sagged into the bed, a slack mess of strung meat.

The lights flickered again. Shadows leapt across the walls, twisting around his bloated, quivering mass. He sniffled, wiping his snot-covered hand across his face again. His weeping filled the room, wet and sticky, until the silence felt heavier, unbearable.

Flynt didn't move. His expression flat, he took a step back away from the bed. His eyes stayed on Godfrey, but there was nothing there.

"Leave me alone," Godfrey whimpered, his voice a croak now, his body curling into itself, folding into the nest of filth beneath him. His head lolled to the side, eyes glazing over.

My footsteps hit heavy, crunching through layers of clothes and trash littering the concrete. The bed sprawled before me, a filthy mound of sagging sheets and torn blankets, the fabric scruffy and stained, fraying off at the edges, crusted with grime and sweat. The air thickened, every breath cloying with the sour stench that clung to the fabric like rot. I leaned against the foot of the bedframe, my knuckles pressing into the sticky, decaying mess.

"Eleanor said—um—that Godfrey would be down here..." My voice came out broken, trembling from somewhere deep in my throat. "She said we'd be safe if we found him—shit—you'd keep us safe." I waited, the words catching in my chest.

Godfrey's bloated face turned to me, his eyes wet and glistening as he blinked in surprise, a glimmer of something crawling over his expression.

"Eleanor?" His gaze drifted over the room. His tongue darted out, slicking his cracked lips. "She's here?"

My stomach twisted, something cold and hard settling in my gut.

"She's dead…" I caught my balance against the sticky, uneven frame. "Eleanor's dead," I said, voice just above a whisper, forcing the words out. His face shifted.

"Oh dear," he muttered, shaking his head. "That's truly sad." It was a smirk. "Poor thing." His eyes lingered on mine, glassy.

The room seemed to tighten; the walls pressed in closer, making each breath feel thin, strangled. I tried to blink, tried to breathe, but the silence held me in place, heavy, suffocating.

"Yamagzhal…" The name slipped out before I could stop it, tearing out of me in a cracked whisper. "She…she killed her. Yamagzhal's here." My knees felt weak, my legs shaking as though the floor tipped under my feet.

Godfrey's face froze, his eyes flicking down and then back up. His lips twitched.

"Yamagzhal?" His voice slipped into something whiny. "That's it?" He gave a wet, wheezy laugh, his gaze empty, bored. His flesh pressed into the mattress, every inch of him spilling into the decaying nest of fabric.

I remained looming over him, my chest heaving. The air shuddered with each of my breaths, hot and heavy in the cold stillness of the room. I fixed my gaze on the chipped concrete beneath my shoes, my shadow pulsing with the flicker of the light.

The rhythm of my heart hammered in my ears, a drumbeat drowning out the soft swing of the bulb above. It cast an erratic glow that played tricks on my vision, turning the stained floor into a shifting tableau of grime and fear.

Godfrey shifted, his bulk casting a heavy shadow across the tangle of blankets. His eyes found Braelyn in the gloom, her form crumpled against the cold steel.

"Braelyn." The word was soft, laced with a tenderness that seemed out of place amidst the decay. "Braelyn…" he said again, each syllable trembling through the stifling air.

My boots scraped on the littered floor, my movements stiff. My breath was still uneven, my hands curled into fists at my sides. Godfrey reached out, a hesitant gesture toward the motionless figure.

"Braelyn…" His voice wavered with a note of humanity. The light bulb swung gently, its dim glow casting eerie shadows that danced over Braelyn's stillness. My jaw clenched, the muscles tight and trembling.

Braelyn twitched. A feeble hand rose, palm grazing the wire mesh, fingers trembling. Eyes blinked open, glinting dully in the flickering light. Her body convulsed, a grotesque dance against the pull of gravity. Limbs quaked and folded, then, with a surge of will, propped her into a sitting heap.

Black bile oozed, thick and shining, from the gaping maw torn through her jaw. It pooled on the concrete, mingling with the detritus beneath her. The stench hit the air, a foul, metallic tang that clung to the back of my throat.

Braelyn's gaze lifted. Hollow eyes met Godfrey's. No words. Just a stare, heavy and expectant.

"Where's Eleanor?" Godfrey's voice broke the silence, soft as a whisper, yet heavy with an edge of urgency.

Braelyn met his question with silence. Her eyes, dark and empty, fixed on him. Time stretched thin between us. Tears formed. They gathered like dew, brimming at the edge of her eyelids. One slid down, cutting through the grime on her cheek, leaving a clean trail in its wake. Another followed, then another—silent streams carving paths over her skin. The room held its breath.

Godfrey watched her—body still, eyes locked; his smirk pulled into a narrow grin. The light above swung gently, casting a quivering shadow that played across Braelyn's tear-stained face. Godfrey cleared his throat, a guttural sound that seemed to echo off the walls. His eyes locked onto Braelyn's, probing, insistent.

He shifted, the movement awkward and graceless. His gaze dropped to his own paunch, then flicked back to the figure before him. A pointed finger shook as it aimed at her. His voice wavered.

"You see those clothes you're on?" His eyes darted from the pile beneath her to her face again. "Could you get those for me?" The request hung in the air.

Braelyn's tears ceased. Her eyes went barren. A dull gaze dropped below her. Hands trembled as they brushed against the fabric heap, searching, feeling the grimy textures.

She found purchase; fingers curled around a clump of stained cotton, tugging it free from the refuse. The pile shifted, releasing its hold with a soft hiss.

She launched the tangled mass across the room. It sailed, a dirty trail of dust. The ball of clothes struck the concrete with a thud, rolling to a halt at Godfrey's feet. Godfrey's hands closed around the bundle. Fabric squished between thick fingers.

"Thank you, Braelyn," he murmured, the words oddly tender.

Braelyn staggered back toward her heap by the door, sagged to the ground, and dropped her head back. Cold metal of the elevator grating pressed into her scalp. Each breath a shallow rasp, each blink slow, deliberate. She was still, save for the quiver of an involuntary shudder. The green metal star lay flat on the pant leg of her uniform.

Godfrey heaved, his mass shifting. The bed groaned beneath him as he rose, a pale mountain of flesh. His belly, a fleshy overhang, quivered with the effort. Naked, he stood towering on the stained mattress.

One leg lifted, hovered, plunged into beige denim. Balance wavered. The frame creaked, threatening to splinter under his dance. Godfrey's gaze swept the room, eyes glassy, locking onto mine for a half-beat.

The other leg found its way. Fabric swallowed the skin. He yanked up the jeans, fumbling with the button. A tug, a zip, the rasp of metal teeth meshing.

He fished a sweatshirt from the bundle—blue, grid-striped. Arms burrowed through sleeves. Head popped out the neck hole. He tugged it down, fabric stretching over his girth. Zipper sealed the last of his exposed flesh from view.

My fists clenched at my sides until my knuckles felt ready to split open. Godfrey's bulk dropped onto the edge of the bed, the frame stretching under him with a low, pained groan. His feet slapped the concrete, toes gripping it. He heaved himself upright, shoulders rolling to catch his balance in the dim, uneven light.

I closed in, the air between us thick and close. His head turned, gaze settling on me, eyes steady, almost glassy, gleaming with something dark. He waited, his mouth twitching, a stale, smug smell bleeding into the gap between us.

"She knew how to find a door," he began, voice scraping out. "Slipped right through when things got hard, didn't she?" His fingers wandered to his waist, dragging under his belt, inching lower, before scratching down, deep and slow. He shifted his weight, letting the scratch go on, his nails biting hard through the fabric. He took his time with it. "Guess she's not coming back though. Left some things behind, sure. Some promises she never had any business making."

He let his hand drop, the sound of skin against his thigh thick in the stale air. He looked up, sweat sheening his face, beads clinging along his jaw. His mouth curled—just a suggestion of it—as his eyes stayed pinned to me.

"It's funny, the ones who stick around. Those who try." His voice dropped lower, dripping, each word slow, deliberate. "But the ones that stay, they never seem to matter in the moment, do they?" A glance past me, toward the door where Braelyn's shadow hung useless and slack. "Always waiting to pick up your mess."

The bulb flickered above, casting thin black shadows that snapped across his face, across the room. Braelyn stood in the corner, her uniform collar catching thick streaks of black sludge oozing from her mouth. She kept still—left it streaked across her face.

I shifted, jacket scraping against the wall. Godfrey's gaze flicked down, then back up, scrutinizing every inch like he was seeing something rotten. His stare dug in, flat and unblinking.

"I understand that when someone's got nowhere else to go, they take what they're given." His lips crept apart, each word cutting. "That kind of kindness—it doesn't come easy." He waited, letting the words fester, letting their weight hang in the space between us. "Can be hard to see, though, when someone's too wrapped up to notice. Too busy needing everything."

He shifted, scratching his side again—digging deeper this time. "Some people keep trying though," he went on, voice a rasp, each word dragging out. "Never enough though. Not for the ones who don't want it." He let his eyes settle on me, holding the silence, a breath away from pressing further.

Then he exhaled, an ugly, sour breath filling the gap. "Guess there's always some of us stuck with it all in the end—the inheritance of guilt." He whispered it, his grin sour and faint. "Guess you already know."

The words struck cold, sickly. His stare never wavered; every inch of his bulk settled heavy, his weight pressing down on each word. He watched me with a persistent stillness. "That's just the return."

Godfrey's bulk shifted, the bed creaking as he stood. I watched him, gaze lingering, then broke the silence, voice halting.

"What is—what's that shit mean?"

He paused, head cocked in a glassy stare.

"The recurrence," he murmured, voice thin, brittle. "Waves against the shore, endless. Breaking against what's left, wearing it down and returning the pieces." His words settled like dust, each one soft but pressing down with a dull weight.

"The return," he continued, his gaze drifting back to me, "is broken, filthy. It watches as it grinds you down." He moved a step closer, his voice just above a whisper. "Those who remain rot until they've been hollowed out." His gaze landed on Braelyn in the corner, the thick black sludge creeping down her jaw, staining her collar.

"They lose pieces," he said, voice so soft it almost didn't reach me. "Left with just enough to walk around, but barely worth the space they fill. They're barely people—you'd never call them that if you saw what was left." His words dripped, disgust pooling underneath, heavy and thick. He waited, gaze pinned to me, as though expecting an answer. I swallowed, my voice a whisper.

"Hey. So, if the return gives back what's left…" My head tilted, gaze slipping to the edge of the room. I stumbled into a murmur. "If I let someone die, or if I killed them…" My voice wavered into a flat whine, teeth clenching tight. "If the return gave back what's left of Gary—can I have him back?"

"Forget about him. Gone is gone." Godfrey's voice cut through the air, sharp and final. His stare didn't soften. "Get over it." His calm was frigid, smooth.

I froze, throat tightening, but as I pulled my gaze away, something sharp crawled up my leg. I jolted, looking down, pulling at the hem of my jeans. Dark vines, wet and pulsing, were twisting under the skin, winding around bone and muscle, sprouting small black roses with dark, sickly petals. Thorns pressed into my leg, piercing through, dragging tiny trails of blood that slid over my ankle. I tried to flex my foot, but the vines gripped tighter, twisting with a slow, wet pull.

Godfrey watched, his face unchanged. I clamped my jaw against the pain, but my fingers prickled, something pushing under the nails. I looked down, watching as more of the vines crept from beneath, black thorns pressing out the nails, sliding through the skin. My blood ran warm over my knuckles, dripping down my wrist. Godfrey's silhouette loomed, a dark shape against the flickering light.

"Why did you come here?"

"We were hungry," I muttered, voice rough, fists clenched until my knuckles paled. Flynt's eyes flashed, his face impassive. The bulb swung above, casting erratic shadows that danced across the crumbling walls.

"Oh my—oh dear," Godfrey whispered, his voice thin and meek, unfitting his hulking frame. "How rude of me. Here, for you." His heavy steps echoed against the concrete. He stopped, bending over, his shirt lifting to reveal rolls of slack, damp flesh along his lower back. He reached toward a small black mini-fridge pressed against the grime-slick wall, its surface wet and oozing, black trails slipping down its edges. Grunting, he wrenched it open, reaching in with thick, meaty fingers. A pale shape emerged from the dripping darkness—a white cat, segmented and twisted, stiff in death. Half-fused heads drooped between the legs, tiny mouths rigid, wide black eyes staring blankly.

Godfrey turned, the thing draped across his forearm, limp and sagging. Its fur was soft and matted only at the edges, streaked with yellow bile. I felt hunger gnaw at me, even as bile crept up my throat. Flynt's gaze stayed fixed. Braelyn's eyes opened wide, locked on the cat with ravenous intensity.

Braelyn's fingers clawed at the metal grate as she dragged herself upright, her torn cheeks fluttering like tattered flags. Dark blood soaked through her uniform, weaving across the faded cotton as her fingers clenched and scraped across the grate. Her wide, glittering eyes stayed on the cat, the gleam of hunger unmistakable.

His thumb dug into the creature's back, pressing until the flesh twisted, bone giving way with a sharp crack. The air filled with a sickly, wet pop as he broke off a small leg, the white fur glistening with dark patches. Braelyn lurched forward, her jaw slack, blood braiding like black ribbons as her gaze fixed on the limp, mangled cat.

The smell hit hard, thick and metallic, filling the room with a putrid stench that clawed up my nostrils. I braced myself, feeling the hard concrete beneath me, each breath shallow and sharp. Flynt and Braelyn stood close on either side of me, their breaths mingling with the sour air, gaze never wavering.

"What's that?" Flynt's voice broke through, low, indifferent.

The broken creature swayed in Godfrey's hand, its twisted segments shifting, half-formed heads and legs suspended. I turned slowly, grinding my boots against the filthy floor, watching Flynt's gaze linger on the cat.

"It's…a cat," I muttered, voice tumbling into a rasp. "My brother has one…"

My words faltered as a chill swept the room, tightening my jacket against my shoulders, the walls seeming to close in. Overhead, the flickering bulb shuddered, casting shadows that jerked and twisted with each biting draft. Godfrey barely looked, his face impassive as he turned the lifeless cat in his hands.

"They can't feel anything on their own. They don't think—Nazhals, I mean. They don't need to," he murmured, voice low and almost amused. "They watch, they imitate. Drawn to whatever shines the brightest, whatever they can latch onto." His eyes slid to mine, a faint, bitter smile at the edges. The bulb swung again, casting his face in harsh relief as he tore another segment off the cat's body, each break punctuated by the wet crunch of bone.

"Are they good?" Flynt's voice cut through the cold, flat and dry.

Godfrey cradled the stiff, unnatural cat-thing with strange tenderness, his pudgy fingers pressing deep into the white fur, caressing the fur that lay soft against his thumb. He twisted slowly, deliberate, savoring each break as bone cracked, filling the room with a sharp crunch that burrowed under my skin.

Godfrey tore another piece, the crunch reverberating in the small space, thickening the air. I swallowed hard, feeling the stench of rot creep deeper, clinging to the walls, settling heavy in my throat.

He brushed a fleck of meat from his moustache with one thick thumb, wheezing through his nose. "They aren't human. Not Flynt, not Braelyn, not Eleanor—" his greasy tongue clicked against the roof of his mouth, teeth small and yellowed "—Yamagzhal. They're all the same. Don't ever cry for them." He picked at the edge of his nail, flakes drifting down to the concrete floor. "Oh, and speaking of Yamagzhal— she saw you in front of the station. You brought her with you."

The vines twisted up my arm, blood trickling as they coiled tight, roses blooming between thorns. The scent of rot thickened, each pulse a dull throb under my skin, filling the room with a smell both sweet and vile.

Godfrey lifted a chunk of raw, bloody fur from the dismembered pile—a cat's leg, jagged and stiff, its fur matted with congealed black. He handed it to Braelyn first. Her fingers shook as she gripped it, her throat convulsing as she forced down a chunk. Next, he passed a thicker piece to Flynt, who took it slowly, holding the meat before him, almost admiring it. His mouth opened, deliberate, biting deep into the sinew. Blood trickled from his lips, pooling at his chin, but he chewed without pause, eyes distant.

Finally, Godfrey held out a piece to me. A malformed lump—an underdeveloped skull clung to stringy tendons, eyes faintly reflective in their sockets. I took it, feeling its weight in my palm, staring down at its vacant face. I didn't move, didn't breathe. Braelyn jammed the hunk into her mouth, forcing the meat into the jagged gap where her jaw had split open. Flesh caught on broken teeth, black blood smearing her uniform as her head jerked forward, her throat bulging with each brutal gulp.

"Yamagzhal," Godfrey muttered, his voice threading through the sickly silence. "The Nazhal who watches the return."

But the words faded. A blast filled the room, vibrating through the walls. A horn blasted through—a train—a shudder riding the walls. Everything else fell silent under its weight. The floor heaved, shivering.

The elevator groaned, metal shrieking as Yamagzhal's shadow trickled out of the dark, monstrous limbs unfolding. Braelyn staggered back, tripping over the edge of a chair. Her foot caught, and she went sprawling forward, smashing against the floor. Teeth scattered, brittle pieces clattering, her jaw cracking wider, the ragged gap tearing open farther.

Behind her, the monstrous black chicken in the elevator convulsed, feathers matted with ichor. Yamagzhal's form held upright, looming, a grotesque figure dripping with dense, tarry sludge. The chicken stared up, wings stretched wide, its dark, empty eyes curious, almost defiant. Then the walls of the elevator shifted—unfolding, tearing open like an eyelid peeled back. Hinges screeched, metal grinding as the walls yawned wide, splitting the bird in two. Its body wrenched apart, each half slapped wetly against opposite sides, spraying thick ropes of blood and slop in every direction.

I lurched back as black blood surged across the floor, spreading in a thick, hot sheet, inching around my feet. The air stung, heavy with rust and rot, filling my lungs with every sharp inhale. A dense, suffocating presence, Yamagzhal's shadow stretched long across the room, her form a grotesque silhouette against the stuttering light.

My fingers ached, the vines squeezing tight, winding up past my wrists, thorns pressing, sharp and wet, blood staining my arms. Godfrey's gaze never wavered, his face a vacant mask untouched by rot.

CHAPTER 9:

In front of me, where Godfrey's bed had pressed against the back wall, there was a broad window opening out into the sky above. It churned with streaks of pale gray—thick splotches spiraling along a running canvas.

Black vines coiled tight across my limbs—shriveled, glossy, splotched with streaks of orange blood. It sizzled where it touched, smoke curling from the splits. Cobwebs clung to the outer strands—dry, stringy black growths. I writhed, pressed against a layer of sticky clothes beneath me, and the vines snapped—one by one—until I pulled myself to my feet. The vines slid down my body, slicing fresh slits into my arms as they plopped onto the concrete—wet, limp, and steaming into mush.

The room ahead lay naked. Smooth concrete walls stretched around me; a single light bulb dangled overhead, swaying gently on its wire. Clothes littered the floor, soaked in patches of black and white resin, sticking to the concrete in wet clumps. The corners were bare—the bed was gone, as was the fridge—leaving behind the empty frame of space. The elevator stood behind me, quiet at the far end of the hall.

My eyes fixed on the gulf behind the back wall—a cliff edge. Beyond, the black ocean sprawled to eternity: still, silent, inky waters melding with the dark horizon.

I stepped forward, inching toward the void. Each step I took kicked up a colorful mire. Fabric twisted around my boots, clinging with wet desperation. Sour, it clawed its way into my sinuses.

Colors swirled beneath me, all smeared with dark stains, all spoiled. I nudged a striped shirt with my toe—the fabric sodden and heavy, drowning in absence.

My breath came shallow, quick. The air tasted stale, tinged with mold and something fouler. The clothes whispered as they shifted, their voices rising through the hollow where the furniture had been.

Finality pooled at the drop. I peered over, teetering on the brink. It was empty—just the abyss staring back, unblinking.

The breeze carried salt and rot. My jacket fluttered, the sound sharp against the stillness. Brine touched my lips; dampness clung to my skin.

Tremors split across my spine. My hand brushed my jacket pocket, the fabric rough under my fingertips.

The sky—a confused fresco—bled into the concrete. It wormed its way in like melting glass. Gray clouds churned, thick and oppressive. They spiraled lazily, as if stirred, stripped of hope and despair.

I stepped closer to the jagged break where the station sheared off, where fabric teetered over the drop. A sweater dangled, half over the edge, its fibers frayed, reaching out with desperate fingers before dropping silently into the abyss.

I stood at the seam, my shadow hanging over the fall. Now, there was only the drop.

The ocean below mirrored the sky above—two vast grays—meeting at the world's end. I reached down, my hand brushing against the cloth that crumbled under my touch. I plucked at the garments—the colors dimming under the weight of the sky.

My foot crunched down, something brittle giving way beneath my boot. A tide of insects spilled out from the violated garment. Mites swarmed through the rags blanketing the floor—tiny bodies nestling into the skin-oiled weave. They scurried across the walls.

In the corner of my vision—motionless flesh—his cast-off shell, Godfrey's emptied husk. His body sprawled near the precipice, skin pale against the dark canvas of decay. The tide's memory climbed the rock, lapped against him—but he was already beyond it.

I stepped closer, each movement tentative. The mites swarmed over his form too, a creeping shroud on his nakedness. There was no dignity.

My gaze lingered on the man. My hand twitched. A chill settled deep in my teeth, unshaken by the musty warmth of the room.

The ocean below stretched eternal, awaiting the fall. I looked away, back to the world, away from the edge where the return whispered with the sound of the sun.

Tears streaked Braelyn's face, salt and sorrow mingling. Her hands, trembling with grief and revulsion, clawed at the edges of raw tissue. Godfrey's death-mask of a face stared beyond the horizon as she knelt beside his skin. Her sobbing filled the ocean's hush.

She leaned over, her head resting against his cold side. The mites crawled, indifferent to her anguish, to the desecration. Her fingers dug into his flesh. Teeth gritted, she bit down.

Braelyn's jaws worked frantically, pulling at sinew and tissue. She tore away a mouthful—clumpy orange blood. Organs spilled onto the ground. More followed, her hands reaching, yanking out viscera that squelched between her fingers. The room echoed with each rip and tear from her breaking spirit.

The fabric beneath her knees soaked up the spreading stain, blood and life intermingling. I stood a frozen witness to the weeping, its misery drowning the sky.

Braelyn's hands plunged deeper, a frenzy in the rancid cavity. Ceramics clinked against her fevered search. She drew out jagged shards, each piece etched with stains of Godfrey's blood. Her fingers tightened around them, knuckles white.

Chunks of ceramic filled her grip. Sharp edges bit into her palms, her own blood mingling with Godfrey's. Black droplets fell, swallowed by the concrete.

She gathered more. Her flesh gave way, black ichor seeping from new wounds. Fists clenched, she held the stained fragments close.

The air filled with the quiet rush of her bleeding.

Braelyn's hands shook as she lifted a shard to the light. A pair of lips curved from the glaze, stiff and parted; black hair inked across the arc of a broken shard. Another piece bore half an eye, split clean through the iris—hollow, staring. Blue fabric clung to a distant fragment, cracked where the paint had dried and lifted. My breath hit the air in bursts; mites scattered along the walls. The fragments lay before her—jagged pieces of Eleanor. She arranged them with trembling care—she was missing too many parts.

Near the cliff's edge, Flynt stood. His gaze stretched across the ocean void. Motionless, save for the steady rise and fall of his chest. Sandals teetered over the end of human suffering—yet he remained rooted, a statue carved of apathy. The sea whispered below, but Flynt heard nothing, saw nothing beyond the expanse.

A glint caught my eye, the dim light bulb overhead casting a feeble sheen amidst the color and gunk. I leaned closer. My hand shot out, fingers plunging into the cold, sloshing filth. The fabric clung to my skin, squelching as I sifted through the decaying mess. My fingertips scraped against the rough concrete. Thin steel pricked my skin, a dull, numbing sting. I nudged at it—fingers slick, shaking—but it slipped deeper into the mess.

I squatted, the cold concrete beneath me softened by a cushion of soaked garments. Tar clung to the fabric. It oozed between my fingers as I dug through the mess. The mites swarmed, a living skin over decay.

I gripped a shirt, yanking it aside. More clothes followed in rapid succession—soggy jeans, a ruffled dress, all slick with oily filth. Toxic fire slipped into my pores where the fluid clung. The mites ascended, emboldened by the heat from my frantic movements. They crawled up my arms, tiny feet prickling, drawing lines of revulsion that danced along my nerves. I flinched, shook my limbs, but they clung.

Scraps tore from the floor—ripped free from each other with soppy resistance. The garments peeled upward, slow and sticky, revealing a static pool of sky beneath the concrete. My breath clouded the air before the chill swallowed it.

A small, jagged intruder met my fingertips amidst the slick. I snatched at it, a green metal earring emerging from the poison. The tiny glint caught my eye as I brushed it off on my jacket, the cold metal prickling against my skin.

It was a green star, its surface reflecting the wavering light. The chill of the room seeped into the metal, turning it icy against my skin. I shoved the earring into my inside jacket pocket—my hand stopped trembling, if only for a moment. It pressed against my chest through the fabric of my jacket.

As I rose to my feet, another glint caught my eye. Sunlight bled orange across the black ocean's expanse, its eerie dance on the still waters painting a sickly dawn. The chill that had threaded deep into my ribs now gave way to a suffocating dry-heat. I squinted against the glare into the five intertwining suns that branded my eyelids—stitched Godfrey into my memories.

The room hummed with the energy of the light, mites retreating into plaster splits. Sweat beaded on my forehead, dripped down my spine. My clothes stuck to my skin. The jacket dragged at my shoulders, bound me, fused.

The five suns twisted through one another in slow, grinding orbits. They pulsed—blood-bright, wet with light—spilling orange fire across the black ocean. Each beat shimmered on the surface, flares skittering through the tide, frying the water where they touched. Their glow burned upward, pressed through the roof, blistered the walls. Heat thickened. Blood-light pooled in the corners. Godfrey, clawed free from the shell and the empty room, had risen past heat and weight and skin. His hearts turned overhead. His eyes bled into the station.

It was him—the five suns bound in chainlight, smeared across the sky, wound in gauze. They turned with slow intention; each orbit dragged heat through itself, folding light into a thick film. My reflection bled from his lantern-light—five pupils burning against the canvas sky, their glow soft at the edges, hot with knowing; he swallowed me without motion, his heat branding me in an instant. The sky curved around him, bent in reverence—the end of the eternal recurrence, the end of human suffering—Godfrey.

A distant sound scratched at the edge of my awareness—a cry, low and mournful, spiraling up. It pulled at me through the silence that had settled over the room. My head turned, hair sticking to my cheeks.

I took an involuntary step toward the sound, my shoes crunching on the colorfully stained, rancid mess beneath my feet. The mites scattered between my legs, exposing the starving concrete.

The sobbing grew in volume, yet remained distant, carried on winds that stirred from somewhere beyond the room. My hands clenched, nails digging into my palms. The earring sank into my flesh through the pocket's lining.

My gaze fixed on the black ocean beneath and the gnarled sky above.

My breath came out in short bursts, my chest tight as the air slid its hand down my throat. I held onto the cries—dragged them with me.

My muscles tensed. I stepped backward, slow, pulled inexorably toward the source of the sound. My shadow stretched long behind me, fractured by the radiant light—sharp and blistering—etched black across the drop.

I spun on my heel; the sound wrenched me from the ocean. The hallway waited before me. Wallpaper clung to the concrete walls in loose patches; faded flowers speckled the surface. Flakes curled from the seams. At the far end stood a wooden door—brown, paneled, bedroom-style. From behind it, the sobbing leaked through the frame, thin and scraping, clawing at the air.

My steel-toes struck wet concrete, the cry echoing, lacing itself around my spine. I stumbled, righting myself with a palm against the peeling wall. Dust clung to my jacket, mingling with the sweat at my nape.

I reached the door, my shadow erratic in the dim light. Hands—traitorous, shaking—grasped the cold knob: twisted, pushed, pulled. The metal groaned. My fingers worked frantically, nails scraping against the surface. The weeping threaded through my fingers.

The sobbing swelled beyond the door. I recoiled, then hammered my fists against the wood, the thuds hollow.

"Open the door!"

White knuckled, I clawed at the doorframe. Wood splintered beneath my nails, fine dust falling into ash on the hardwood. Skin split at my fingertips, blood welling and dripping to the floor in dark, spattered droplets.

"I was just joking. I was being stupid, and—"

I kicked at the base, feet pounding the swollen paneling—again and again, a rhythm to match the heart on the other side. My breath rasped, the taste of static thick in my nose.

"Please… Please don't."

Tears scorched trails down my cheeks. They soaked my collar. My jaw trembled, throat frayed.

"I'm sorry," my voice cracked.

"I'll really quit this time, please!" I pounded again, harder. My blood streaked the wood.

"Please let me in!" A sob caught in my throat, a strangled thread of hopelessness.

Silence swallowed the sobs on the other side. I slumped, forehead pressed to the cool surface. The hush of stillness pressed around me. Sweat gathered at the nape of my neck.

"Don't scare me like that," I whimpered. Bedsprings settled beyond the door—gliding across the empty room. "I love you."

The floorboards creaked beneath my shifting weight. "I still… I—" Dust motes danced in the sliver of light that penetrated the curtains.

"Please…" My hands streaked down the door. "Please! Please!" My chest lurched; I choked on spit and tears.

A gunshot thundered from behind the door.

My heart stopped, then burst. I staggered back from the door. The room froze. Plaster dust drifted from the ceiling. My breath caught on the vacancy.

My gaze locked onto the doorframe, waiting, but the room was empty. The wood was still. The fabric had been silenced.

My hand hovered in the air, fingers still curled as if around the doorknob. Copper lingered on my tongue. I stood motionless. Outside, the world held its breath. The quiet had ensnared me. The echoes of our pleas had vanished.

The gunshot's echo decayed, leaving behind a dense hush that pressed against my eardrums. My ears strained, drawing in the stagnant breath of the hallway, searching for life, for change.

But there was none.

My legs buckled. I crumpled, my shoulder hitting the door with an echoing thud. My voice sealed away within tight lips. Silence draped my skin—warm and damp.

I slid down, the wood grain rough against my jacket. A squatting shadow at the base, the cold seeped through my clothes, grounding me to the spot.

My hands trembled as they rose—slow, deliberate. Palms grazed my cheeks, fingers traced the lines of my jaw. The skin was wet, salt-streaked. My fingertips passed over my face—barely there.

My eyes clamped shut. The dark, the world outside, the throbbing silence—they were gone. Breath shallow, quivering—a struggle past a constricting throat.

The side of my head rested against the door. Fabric softener and clotted rust strangled the hall. The room spun.

My shoes dug into the old hardwood. My fingers clawed at my face. A bead of blood wound its way down my wrist.

Tears slipped through my clenched eyelids, trailing down my cheeks. They gathered, cool, at the edge of my chin. Drops fell, one by one, onto my hands. The wetness seeped between fingers, dripping onto the floor.

"I'm sorry—I'm sorry."

My chest rose and fell with ragged force. A whimper escaped my lips. The blurring hardwood darkened with the slow patter of tears.

My knees crumpled against the ground. My hands fell away from my face, limp at my sides. They left pale streaks against my skin.

The door creaked. My head snapped toward the whisper, my eyes wide, searching within the beckoning sliver of darkness.

A chill spilled from the gap, caressed my face. I drew back. The air tasted stale, laced with the must of his old carpet.

I pushed myself up. My knees ached, joints cracking in the quiet. Fingers grazed the door; its surface was cool. It moved again—a breath beneath the surface.

Darkness peered out from the opening, vast and hungry. It reached for me. My breath hitched, swallowed by the void. The carpet beyond rustled. I leaned closer, the tips of my sneakers brushing the threshold.

My hand trembled, reaching for the darkness. My pulse echoed in my ears.

My gaze fixed on the black maw before me. Each muscle tensed, ready to spring. But I remained still, frozen by the slit between door and frame.

My skin prickled. The darkness swelled, pressing against the door. Poised to spill forth, to consume, it brushed against my face.

The silence stretched into a dying breath.

Then, the night exhaled.

CHAPTER 10:

I crawled through the doorway, fingers dragging over the threshold. Carpet scraped against my palms as I heaved myself inside.

I smeared my forearm over my face. Sticky heat clung, itchy where my skin rubbed raw. Salt burned into patches, grit grinding under my sleeve. Silence swelled—thick, pulsing in my skull. My jacket scraped the dry carpet.

The sour slick of mucus coated my tongue; heat scraped my throat, raw and tight. Sweat slid down my spine. My palms pressed to the floor, fibers grinding into my skin. My knees slipped, and my chest hit the floor. Breath rasped against the weave as I hauled myself back to my hands and knees. My fingers scraped along the carpet, catching on threads, rough and fraying.

The air was denser here, suffocating and stale My shoulders twitched. It stuttered overhead—a sharp pulse, stark, white, and searing. It was a brief flash. The shadows stretched long before snapping back.

I froze, one hand hovering above the carpet. The flickering grew frantic, spilling white-hot flashes. The bed was broad, sharp-edged, and unnaturally wide. Covers draped low, brushing the floor. Beneath them, a white cat lay still, its chest rising and falling in a delicate rhythm.

The light died again, and darkness surged back. A low gust rippled through the room, carrying something vile. Above, the fan groaned and rattled. Wallpaper curled at the edges. The faded floral pattern—it was the same—always the same.

The fan sliced through the air above, its blades catching the flickering light. A creak groaned through the house. Heat radiated from beneath my fingertips. Something shifted—small, just out of reach.

Another flicker—my gaze snapped to the bed again. It might have been empty. The light wouldn't hold still. I clenched my teeth, aching and grinding.

My hand reached out and brushed something cold—a bedpost. I yanked back, the chill biting into my palm. The wood was dry and smooth, yet my skin throbbed where it touched me. I edged along the side of the bed, muscles taut, breath shallow. Another burst of light tore through the dark—then gone. The darkness clamped down.

I craned my neck upward. Beside the bed, its skin was pale and sponge-like, riddled with layers of winding holes. Black and white streaks dribbled down its skin, splattering the carpet with glossy plops. The stains spread, seeping into the fibers. Tan skin stretched taut over an impossible form. Patches of matted, curly brown hair clung stubbornly to its scalp.

I scrambled backward. My hands slipped in the sticky mess, shoes skidding uselessly against the floor.

The thing wore his clothes.

Black stains streaked the fabric, distorting it, warping it. The faint floral pattern of the wallpaper turned sickly in the strobe. Its face was a honeycomb of pores, seeping foul, acrid juice. The stench tightened my throat, a mix of rot and chemical burn.

I fell hard, my arm jamming against the stiff carpet. The impact numbed me for a moment. My ears rang, warmth dripping down my neck. I wheezed.

"Fuck… Please— No."

The enormity pressed in, folding the room around its neck. A void of sound filled the air; my breath turned shallow, my chest buckling under the weight.

I clawed at the ground, fingers brushing the bedpost. I gripped it. Wood bit into my palm as the world tilted, splintering under the pressure. I could see myself in the eclipse.

Tears streamed down my face for the loss of what I'd become, everything I'd destroyed.

The strobe was a metronome. Thin fingers, like saplings, writhed free from the skin, grasping at the air and then their host.

My heart stopped, locked by the collapse of Yamagzhal—the return, swallowed in a cycle of suicide. I shuffled backward, the base of my palm pressing into the soft weave.

More fingers clawed out, bursting from its face—jagged roots shredding flesh and soil. They tugged, snapping strands of cobweb flesh. The sinew popped—wet, sharp.

Sweat beaded on my forehead, mingling with tears. I refused to remember. The taste of salt on my lips, I watched, paralyzed, as it mutilated itself.

Its face ruptured. A jagged seam split the head down the middle, skin peeling back in moist shreds. Each half slumped onto its respective shoulder, gushing white bile that stained its shirt and pooled on the floor.

I staggered back, throat tightening, lungs failing. The strobe splintered the room into jagged flashes—its fingers ripping, tearing at itself.

From the gaping neck slit, two pale, porous arms emerged. They reached out, grasping the body's sides. The snapping of bones was a deep resonance that vibrated down my throat.

Its torso split, charred organs spilling free with heavy plops. They struck the carpet with a squelch; milky fluids spread around them in sluggish pools. Wet bile surged up my throat and splashed onto the floor, orange against the carpet.

It stood, the halves of it dangling at its sides. I tried to flinch. I tried to blink.

Yamagzhal unfolded. Black blood and entrails smeared patterns into the carpet.

My heart hammered against my ribcage. I pressed my back against the wall, cold sweat slicking my spine. The air stank of iron.

It turned—a jerky, unbalanced pivot. It faced the bed. The ceiling fan above cast a stuttering light, carving each movement into still frames. Yamagzhal swayed.

I clenched the carpet, tearing loose thick strands. The pressure bit back, nails splitting, skin ripping, as the fibers refused to give.

Yamagzhal's silhouette dominated the room. I stifled a sob—the sound strangled in my throat.

The bed ruffled. Fabric pulled tight, then released, as something stirred beneath. A series of muffled creaks scraped along the stillness.

The blankets bunched, shifted, then peeled back. Pale fingers slipped out, knuckles taut, trembling as they gripped the edge. The covers dragged back. Godfrey crawled out, his spine arched, shoulders jutting under his damp skin, ribs rising with shallow, uneven breaths.

Godfrey's eyes were wide, the whites stark in the fractured light. His face was otherwise slack and empty. He scrambled backward, his spine slamming into the hard edge of the bedframe. The mattress sagged beneath him. Blankets bunched in his fists, trembling where they pressed against his bare chest.

It towered above the inheritance of guilt. The mask stared downward: thick white ceramic. Black marker traced uneven circles into the eyes, scrawled overtop each other until the edges blurred. The mouth stretched wide, ink bleeding in jagged streaks. It tipped. The motion was slow but unstoppable. The mask slid free and dropped. Time stretched thin as it fell.

Godfrey whimpered under the covers, tears carving clean paths through the sweat on his cheeks.

It loomed over the man. Its head sagged, flat and misshapen. Black hair hung in oily strands, dripping down its legs. Wrinkled skin bunched tight around the hole—a wet, bumpy maw. Moist edges puckered, breathing. The hollow face fixed itself on Godfrey. Behind it, the void rippled, devouring light. The air and silence grew brittle, beginning to crack.

My breath was shallow. My chest tightened with Godfrey's muffled sobs. Every muscle coiled tight, twisting and strangling, choking my body in place.

Black drool rolled down its chin, splashing on the floor with an inky thud. My heart thundered in my ears as the juice rooted itself into the carpet like veins.

The center of Yamagzhal's face split. Flesh stretched outward in puckered, straining folds, tearing into moist flaps that peeled back with sharp, wet cracks. Thin strands snapped, collapsing into the void, as its skin pulled back across its skull. Loose folds trembled at the edges, sagging under the strain. Black ropes of fluid seeped from the ruptures, pooling on its chin before dripping in sticky streams that hissed into the floor. The fluid misted faintly in the air, clinging to the edges of the expanding void in glossy streaks.

Fingers erupted in spasms—a writhing mass of charred black digits, some thick and gnarled, others impossibly thin and needle-like. Brittle flakes scattered as they forced their way free, its splitting skin leaking tar in steady streams. They coiled and spiraled in impossible patterns, knotting together, splitting apart, and folding back on themselves before straightening in violent bursts. They folded into themselves, twitching and churning; sharp edges tore at tar-slick skin, their rhythm jagged.

A blunt finger punched through Godfrey's skull. Bone cracked, his head slamming into the wall, rattling the room. His skull popped, orange pulp spraying against the wall in thick, glistening streaks. Blood exploded outward, streaking across the bedframe and broken floorboards.

The fingers didn't stop. They shoved in clusters—a writhing black growth, crushing bone, snapping muscle, and shredding skin. His face folded inward around the churning stalks, skin pulling taut before ripping apart in wet, jagged strips. Teeth shattered, fragments ricocheting off the splintered frame.

They drove deeper, smashing through his chest and twisting upward. Splinters of jawbone and shards of rib embedded in the fractured wall, cutting into the pulp-stained surface. Blood gushed in thick rivers, pooling across the remains of the bed, soaking into torn sheets and broken wood.

Godfrey sagged. Strips of orange flesh hung loose from the writhing stalks that held him pinned to the wall. Below, the floor drowned in thick, glistening blood, spreading out in uneven trails that carved through the wreckage.

The walls peeled; large chunks of surface split apart, sagging like wet meat, before tearing free entirely. The pieces hit the ground with thick, wet slaps, dissolving into puddles of wax that shimmered and flowed outward.

I braced against the pull, dragging myself upright on stiff legs. The gravity hung thick in the room—heavy, low—pressing my knees inward as I rose. An icy wind sheared through the open space, dry and blinding, white-out air that scraped my throat raw. I staggered, boots slipping against resin-slick threads, arms out to steady myself.

Its body froze, then convulsed. Its skin bulged and stretched, pulling taut before splitting. Spirals of black and white fluid dribbled down in uneven trails as the flesh pulled open, rupturing. From each fissure, an eye emerged, glaring wildly in every direction. The eyeballs jerked and twitched, rolling and snapping to focus on Godfrey—something stretched and undone, a hollow distortion of flesh folded into wet ash. White lashes sprouted from the edges of each eye, long and coarse, writhing like pale worms.

More eyes sprouted. They ripped through its skin, glossy and wet, tearing into one another where they overlapped. Blood streaked the crooked flesh; they shredded each other. Its clothes split apart as eyes swarmed overtop the fabric, devouring it in twitching, ceaseless growth.

I stood frozen. The air inside me was sharp and heavy, buzzing through my limbs. My skin prickled as though it was splitting open, but I remained completely still. The ground rolled beneath me, waves with a nauseating lurch, as though something massive shifted beneath the floor. My breath caught, my chest tightening with every shudder of the room. My vision flickered, the edges going black, then returning, filled with the sight of Godfrey—pinned, torn, and lifeless, his body reduced to a pulsing heap beneath the endless writhing mass. But he held—whole beneath it all, untouched and waiting, too vast to break.

My hand brushed against the wall, sinking into the soft, sticky flesh that squirmed beneath my fingernails. I recoiled, wiping my palm on my pants, leaving a streak of dissolving hues. My ears rang with the impossible hum of the light and the soft squelch of Godfrey's dismemberment.

The room dissolved into static, its edges fraying into nothing.

The sucking swelled in the snow. Orange droplets dribbled from Godfrey's shattered chin, pooling on the charred fingernails of the return. The blood trickled upward, twisting a crooked path along the matted fingers.

Godfrey's face collapsed—sucked up the fingers in a tight spiral, skin stretching in slick, translucent sheets along the bundle. His neck cracked, bent back, as his skull thinned and warped, molding to the dripping joints that speared him. Blood slicked his cheeks, ran into the folds, and pooled in the open seams. His body shivered beneath the sweltering sap, the orange glow smearing his mutilated frame under the strobing light.

Tears blurred my vision. I stumbled backward, my heel catching on the unraveling carpet. The threads writhed, peeling away from the floor—beneath, the concrete pulsed with excitement.

I lurched forward toward Yamagzhal, dragging one foot at a time, the carpet sloughing off beneath me in fibrous strips. My palms slapped the concrete, sticky with resin; it throbbed under my weight. Heat coiled in my chest. My throat tightened as I approached her—towering, endless—the eternal return.

"Please… Just—just let me show you," I whispered.

The blood kept rising, a slow, inexorable tide. The blackened fingers throbbed inside his skull, squeezing fresh torrents of blood down Godfrey's cheeks. Thick rivulets streaked his neck, spilling onto his chest. The drops gathered, and they fell in heavy beads onto what remained of the bed.

Godfrey's figure hung limp, dominated by the will of Yamagzhal. He swayed slightly, powerless to stop the birth of another.

A moth emerged. White wings unfurled, stained with carmine specks. It gnawed through flesh with jagged teeth. More followed, birthing themselves from within the skin.

Black mites scurried out of fresh wounds. They danced across Godfrey's pallid skin, weaving in and out of the torn fabric, threads fused with muscles and tendons. Yamagzhal was stuck—tangled in nerves and memories, too deep to cut free.

I recoiled, my boots slipping on the slick floor. My hands flailed. Jagged shapes tore open across my skin, sharp-edged gashes that punched straight through. I lifted my hand, and the floor stared back at me through a perfect, hollow void. The pattern spread, holes ripping through my arms, my legs, my chest. Blood gushed from the edges, dripped thick and fast onto the trembling floor. My arms dangled, useless, shredded.

Cold swept over me, sinking deep into my limbs. My breath hitched; the air was leaden, suffocating. The room pressed down harder, and I doubled over, coughing up a wet splatter of blood that dripped down my chin. My vision blurred, the edges smearing into white streaks. The floor tilted beneath me. I was falling—everything was spinning, weightless.

I dropped hard, my head cracking off the steel of her stop-sign skin. The blow spun me sideways—knees buckling, hands slapping weakly against her ankles. I brought trembling fingers to my scalp, breath catching.

"Stop… Please, just look…" I choked. "You'll feel better. I swear."

Blood spattered. A droplet landed on my cheek, hot and viscous. I brushed it away with trembling fingers.

The room shrank with every pulse of its still-beating heart. Desperation clawed at my throat.

Yamagzhal swarmed, swallowing the room—crushing, endless. Godfrey swayed, his body folded inside-out. Flesh peeled back in glistening layers, the raw insides slick and wet, shimmering with a deep, fleshy orange. Orange muscle fibers pulled tight, some snapping free and hanging like torn rope, slick with thick blood. They glistened, streaked sparsely with swirling patterns of black and white. His skin curled outward in jagged flaps, the edges wrinkled and split, leaking oil in uneven trails that splattered against the trembling floor.

Organs pressed against the thin, twisted remains of his frame, pulsing weakly, exposed to the open air. Blood poured in heavy streams, hitting the ground with a wet, rhythmic slap. Every slight motion sent strands of tissue swaying, their glistening surfaces stretching before finally tearing free, splattering across the walls.

Moths burst from his guts in a chaotic swarm, wings slapping wet muscle and shredded organs. They ripped free in clusters, slick with orange blood that spattered the trembling floor. Their bodies tangled in the air, slamming into walls and strobing light, coating every surface in twitching filth. The swarm thickened, filling the room with a churning cloud.

The bedframe pulsed under my palm, damp and tacky, with streaks of orange blood drying in uneven smears. I gripped the edge, bones straining as the wood buckled. A dresser crashed to the floor, splitting the boards beneath it.

I reached for Yamagzhal's jeans. Tissue sloughed from my wrist as my fingers curled around the seam—slow, shaking. Pressure ballooned inside my head, tight on the right side. My jaw locked. The skin along my eye prickled and stretched. A bolt of steel punched outward through my temple with a crunch; a traffic light followed, rigid and red, dragging wires as it birthed itself from beneath my ear. Half my vision smeared white. The pole dropped—hingeless—and crushed my right leg beneath itself. Blood spilled in a warm quilt down the steel, poured from my scalp in a full gush—staining half my jacket orange.

But I stayed—in the pressure, in the heat, in the cold of the empty room.

The fan groaned, its mount twisting loose. It dropped with a crunch, metal blades embedding into the trembling floor. My gaze locked on Godfrey, but the room unraveled around him. The walls tore apart in uneven strokes, peeling back to reveal jagged holes. Beyond them, the room hung suspended above a flat black ocean. The water stretched, endless and still.

Orange blood filled my eyes, thick and stinging, choking my vision into a shrinking blur. The room pulled away from me, spinning into the impossible curve of the horizon. Wallpaper stripped clean, concrete walls surrounded me—Godfrey's empty room. The carpet dropped out. I hit cold concrete, sprawled across soiled clothes.

Black fingers speared the air, erupting from Godfrey's flesh—winding in and out of him in a maze of joints. They writhed. His skin tore with ease, orange blood spurting in erratic pulses, painting the white sheets. Clumps of organs, slick and glistening, tumbled onto the bed, each landing with a wet thud.

My eyelids fluttered open. Godfrey's throat sputtered—wet, choking. Blood bubbled and spat through a hollowed gasp. The bed creaked under the weight of what it bore. With a final shudder, Godfrey's husk ceased its struggle. His arms fell to his sides, limp. The infestation had set; the sun had spread.

My hands tugged at Yamagzhal's pant leg—shaky, uneven pulls—as I keeled forward, the other pressed flat against my stomach, holding everything in. My forehead rested near her calf.

"Gary… Please, just look," I whispered. "I promise, you'll like it." I coughed—searing, moist—and spat up a string of blood that burned across my tongue, hot as it slipped down my chin.

The wall just past the bed had vanished. Beyond it: the fall, the black ocean bleeding into the night. The horizon bent under Godfrey—five swollen orange suns. They crushed together, spilling their glow over the black ocean. Light slashed the surface, jagged and violent, splitting the water into shuddering bands of orange and black. The suns loomed large, close—pressing down, breaking the horizon into pieces. Their light didn't touch the room.

The husk had become nothing—hollow and drifting, suspended above the bed. Blood rose; it crept from Godfrey's perforated body, up the black appendages that bound him, connected to the suns by strings of spit—filmy, wet, drawn thin and trembling in the heat. The orange stream slipped into the gaping maw at the center of Yamagzhal's face. I recoiled, my feet shuffling on the blood-soaked concrete. I clutched at my throat, nails digging into skin. Yamagzhal jerked—its hands flew to its head, clawing at the squirming fingers that sprouted like vines. Its body convulsed with each grasp, sharp and erratic. She had seen the suns—her flesh branded with Godfrey; the station blistered with it, soaked in him all at once.

A deep, guttural cry swelled from her—a woman's voice, raw and trembling. She loomed tall despite her collapse, her ruined face—a yawning draw-well—shaking, pointing toward Godfrey. Eyeballs dotted her skin, rolling wildly before they burst one by one. Black-and-white spirals streaked down her body, pooling in thick lines on the hardened carpet.

Godfrey flared, his brightness searing into the corners of the room. The walls shimmered, their edges sharpening, breaking apart in stuttering bursts of orange heat.

Yamagzhal's arms jerked upward, clawing at the saplings sprouting from her skull. The black tendrils writhed and pulsed, slick with her spiraling blood. Her nails tore into them, snapping sinew and flesh with wet cracks. One by one, the saplings fell, curling limp and inky on the floor, staining the surface beneath her.

The room crashed, the walls twisting under the weight of her collapse. Lights flickered, choking on their last glimmer. The impact jolted through my legs as I clutched the bedframe, my fingers digging into the splintered wood.

I gasped, choking on blood and the roaring static. Godfrey's body toppled, a splayed sack of flesh. He hit the bed with a wet crack, the frame snapping under his weight. Orange blood streamed from his mangled form, pooling beneath the collapsed bedframe. Limbs twisted, inside-out meat dangling like broken threads. The light from his skin flickered, faint and stuttering.

The fingers splayed out from the hole in her face, writhing like severed branches. They halted suddenly, seizing up in grotesque, jagged formations. Yamagzhal's trembling hands gripped the closest cluster, her nails biting into the slick, black lengths. She pulled, and the fingers came loose with a wet rip.

They slid free in limp, flaccid bundles, dragging tangled clumps of black-and-white organs with them. The flesh clung together like twisted roots streaked with searing orange veins. Fluids spurted from the torn masses—thick, oozing streams that hissed as they struck her melting skin.

Her hands moved faster. Another bundle came loose, then another. Black tendrils stretched taut before snapping, releasing sprays of spiraling blood. The orange streaks burned through her body, carving jagged lines that peeled her flesh in slick, sloughing sheets. Skin slid from her shoulders and arms in wet, heavy sloshes, exposing raw sinew beneath.

She tried to hold herself together, pressing her hands to the gaping holes in her body. It was useless. Her hands trembled as more viscera spilled out—solid black-and-white organs that thudded to the ground like rotting fruit. They twitched and wriggled, their surfaces glistening with black ichor and streaks of orange. The room filled with slaps and splashes as the flood spread, pooling around her knees.

Pieces of Godfrey's body tumbled free from her frame—tiny severed hands, torn-up legs, and shredded chunks of flesh stained with streaks of orange. A dozen heads—eyes hollow—spilled from her chest. The sightless faces struck the floor with dull, meaty thuds, melding together beneath the layers of blood and viscera.

Darkness swallowed the room. Yamagzhal quivered, her body jerking as her hands clawed at her skull. Thick strands of black and white flesh tore free, stretching and snapping like sinew, their ends writhing in the air. Her skin tore away in long, wet ribbons, curling at the edges as fluids poured from the open wounds.

Thick slabs of her flesh sloughed away in black and white, streaked with searing orange. They hit the floor with wet, heavy thuds, spreading an ichor that hissed as it met the air. Yamagzhal clawed at herself, her pale hands painted with oily black streaks.

Her skin melted away in bubbling rivulets, sinking into the quivering heap of blood, organs, and fragments of Godfrey that surrounded her in a growing lake of rot.

Fractured shadows warped her collapsing form. The lights—the lone, hanging bulb—sputtered and died, choking the room in darkness.

Her silhouette jerked once, then slumped. Silence followed—thick and choking, the air heavy with the stench of iron and charred meat. Her limbs sprawled at unnatural angles, the flesh smoldering. Skin blackened and cracked, curling away in ashen spirals. Beneath the burning layers, sinew twisted and popped, molten orange streaks bubbling as they spilled to the floor.

Silence followed. My breath slowed. I strained to hear something— anything.

A deep blackness consumed what remained of the station. My knees gave out. I hit the floor hard, the cold seeping through my skin. My hand slid across something slick and warm.

The room was still. The silence pressed down, solid and unbroken. I dropped to my side, body curling tight. I lay still, waiting for the room to shift again. But it never changed, nor did it cease to be the same empty room.

But a sliver of gray broke through. My legs quaked, knees unsteady. The light seeped in, slow and timid, stretching across the floor. It reached the edge of my foot. Dust curled in lazy arcs where the light fell. The shapes it touched shifted, soft angles that hinted at edges but refused clarity. The black clung to the corners, unmoving. My eyes searched the blur. Everything stood still but hummed faintly, waiting.

The light strengthened, steady now. It brushed my cheek—cold, detached. I stayed still, breathless. A narrow streak caught the ceiling fan's metal, outlining the off bulb beneath it in a faint gray. The shadows sharpened where the light passed. A pale beam stretched across the floor, the wood catching its edge, glinting.

My hand found the curtain's fabric, shaky and bare. I pulled myself up, the curtains slipping free and pooling at my feet. Light flooded in—overpowering, relentless. Dust whirled to life in the brightness. My hand fell. The room stayed still. Everything was quiet, untouched.

The bed stood pristine, the wooden frame a clean, sharp outline against the walls. Shadows clung to the corners, shrinking back as the light grew. Nothing here was out of place. Nothing remained.

I turned. The floorboards were silent, emptied of their usual creak.

The light grew stronger, filling the room. I stood at the center, unmoving, holding the air close. He lay beneath the covers, his body outlined in stillness. Brown curls fanned across the pillow. The sheet clung to his arms, pinned at his sides. I stepped closer. My shadow crept along the floor, brushing the edge of the bed. The silence grew heavy, dense. My lips twitched—quick and slight. Heat burned behind my eyes. The curtain fabric pooled around my feet. Sunlight poured in, relentless and cold, swallowing the shadows whole.

My head sank forward. A sniffle broke as my hands wandered—brushing my face, falling back to my sides. I turned to the door. My fingers hovered, then closed on the cold knob. It was unmoving, but turned with a quiet shift. This time, it opened. I looked back. The bed was empty. The door clicked shut behind me.

The hallway dimmed, the light from the room faltering against its walls. There was no sound, only a distant hum.

My steps pressed into the hardwood. A narrow hall stretched ahead with a door ajar on the left. Mirrors lined the wall. Their surfaces reflected the empty corridor. Lemon oil polish clung to the air.

I paused at the hallway's end, where the space opened wide. To the left, the living room. To the right, the kitchen—its countertops gleamed, stainless and harsh. A glass lamp hung in the center, patterned with fruit. The dim bulb inside cast a swinging cone of light— faint and uneven. The bulb swayed on its wire; dry dishes sprawled, stacked neatly, their edges catching the pale glow.

A black rose rested on the counter. Its petals shone, wet and dripping, streaks of water pooling beneath it. The bloom sat untouched, stark against the sterile quiet.

I turned and stepped into the living room. Light pierced the curtains, streaking the floor with stripes of gray and gold. The couch stood firm—blue and unyielding—on a patterned rug.

It cradled Braelyn. Thin strands of sweaty blonde hair clung to her pale face. Her head tilted, cheek pressed to the couch. The blue blankets draped over her rose and fell with soft, nasally breaths. A faint smile curved her torn lips. The ruin—the shattered jaw, chunks of bone and flesh streaked with black stars—was distant.

The glass hummingbirds on the TV stand caught the growing light, their edges flickering faintly. On the far wall, bookshelves sagged beneath scattered heaps. I weaved between beams of light prying through the window. Dust swirled in lazy spirals, golden in the shifting glow.

Flynt's silhouette cut through the farthest corner of the room. The light poured over the room, but where he stood, it broke. His silhouette swallowed it. He didn't move. His narrow eyes, dark and glassy, fixed on Braelyn.

I eased across the room, weaving between the couch and the chair. My shadow merged with the patterns of light and dark spilling from the curtained windows. Flynt stayed still, his gaze unbroken, his figure untouched by the shifting glow.

I stopped beside the couch. The blue blanket rose in soft pulses; Braelyn slept tucked beneath it, warm and small. The light shifted, washing over the glass hummingbirds on the television cabinet. Their reflections trembled, scattering faint patterns across the wall before stilling again.

I reached into my jacket. My fingers brushed against the coarse fabric, then closed on the earring—a small, cold weight. I drew it out, the green metal catching the dim light as I lifted it. My hand moved steadily to the coffee table just in front of the couch, lowering the earring until it touched down with a soft, precise clink. The silence held.

Flynt's attention shifted back to Braelyn. His head didn't move; only his eyes slid sideways, settling again on the quiet rise and fall of her chest.

I glanced past the TV. Smooth wooden frames tiled the wall behind it—soft brown, warm to the eye. Gary was there, along with the rest of our family. Some were taken inside his house, some from back home. They smiled anyway, for the few that I was in.

I pivoted. The house had splayed out before me, silent now—gone back to sleep. The front door hung ajar. White light spilled through the crack, aggressive and pure. It pooled on the hardwood floor.

My steel toes clicked softly against the wood. My shadow stretched behind me as I approached the door. The light swelled. It reached out—pale fingers brushing my jacket, my jeans, my face.

I blinked against the glare.

Windows flanked the entrance, their curtains drawn but failing to hold back the light. White spilled through the fabric, soft yet insistent, tracing faint patterns on the walls. I paused at the boundary. It filled the cracks in the doorway with something endless. The white glow washed over me, cool and steady.

My hand reached out, fingertips grazing the edge of the door. The wood was cool and splintered under my touch. I pushed gently. The door swung wide; the light swelled as it poured in, blanketing the floor in brilliance.

I stepped over the threshold. The air bit at my skin—neither cold nor warm. It was just sharp. Each step pressed into something unplaceable. The light surrounded me; it pressed close. It filled my lungs.

The door clicked shut.